UNCOMMON TALES

Read on the Run Anthology

Amanda Bergloff
Ed Burkley
Roxanne Dent
Sarah Doebereiner
Laurie Axinn Gienapp
Meagan Noel Hart
June Low
Mary E. Lowd
R. J. Meldrum
Michael Penncavage
Jonathan Shipley
Ginny Swart

Uncommon Pet Tales

Cover design by Elle J. Rossi - http://www.ellejrossi.com

Smoking Pen Press
PO Box 190835
Boise, ID 83719
www.smokingpenpress.com

ISBN-13: 978-1-944289-09-6

First Edition: May 2017

TABLE OF CONTENTS

INTRODUCTION   **5**

A WALK IN THE PARK
LAURIE AXINN GIENAPP   **6**

SILVER LINING
JONATHAN SHIPLEY   **10**

PATIENCE
R. J. MELDRUM   **28**

ADOPTING CATHY
GINNY SWART   **37**

BURNING BRIDGES
SARAH DOEBEREINER   **47**

KATELYNN THE MYTHIC MOUSER
MARY E. LOWD   **52**

THE LITTLEST WEREWOLF
ED BURKLEY   **62**

HELLHOUND
AMANDA BERGLOFF   **68**

THE LOCKET
R. J. MELDRUM   **76**

PRINCE OF PERSIAN
  JUNE LOW   **85**

A DOG CALLED ALFRED
  GINNY SWART   **93**

DOG DAY
  MICHAEL PENNCAVAGE **107**

SCHRODINGER'S OTHER CAT
  LAURIE AXINN GIENAPP **112**

MR. MACCAWBER'S CHRISTMAS TRADITION
  ROXANNE DENT   **122**

A SILENT TRUTH
  MEAGAN NOEL HART **134**

ABOUT THE AUTHORS   **140**

OTHER TITLES PUBLISHED BY SMOKING
  PEN PRESS   **146**

INTRODUCTION

Fifteen short stories involving pets.

But don't think for a moment that you'll "See Spot Run", or that Lassie will save her master who's fallen in the well. Those are common pet tales, and these are Uncommon Pet Tales.

Within this collection, you'll find a little bit of romance, a little bit of revenge, a few ghosts, and some fantasy and magic. You'll find some uncommon pets such as Katelynn, and Mr. MacCawber, and you'll find some uncommon stories, such as *Patience*, and *Schrodinger's Other Cat*. You'll find stories of man's (or woman's) best friend, and stories where the animals are far from friendly. And you'll find some stories that simply refuse to fit into a category.

As always, each story in the Read on the Run series of anthologies is short, to suit your busy lifestyle.

A WALK IN THE PARK

Laurie Axinn Gienapp

IT ALL STARTED when my dog ran away—well not ran exactly. The best he could manage at 12 years old and 20 pounds overweight was a purposeful lumber. But inasmuch as I was 82 years old and had arthritis in both hips, a purposeful lumber was the best that I could manage as well. I imagine the two of us made quite a picture that August afternoon, what with Rusty's long basset ears flopping, and my cane adding a third, off-beat accompaniment to the sounds of my footsteps and his toenails tapping on the sidewalk.

I was wearing my glasses that day when I clipped the leash to Rusty's collar, but apparently I'd missed the metal ring on the collar, or perhaps the clip stuck and didn't close all the way. There was nothing amiss as we walked down the path to the sidewalk, and there was nothing amiss as we walked down the sidewalk to the corner, and there was nothing amiss as we crossed the street and walked down the next block to the park at the end of the street.

The problem began once we entered the park. I had my eye on the shaded path at the west end of the park, and accordingly I turned right. Rusty— well, I don't know what it was that caught his eye, but whatever it was, he turned left. And I found myself holding a dog-less leash, watching my aging, overweight basset hound lumber away. So of course I followed.

There we were, Rusty running away, and me chasing after him. At least that's how it was in my head, and Rusty's head as well, I think. Except that to the casual observer I suppose it probably looked like I'd brought my dog to the park and unclipped his leash, and we were both strolling along at approximately the same, slow pace, with the dog staying just a bit ahead of its owner.

We passed some children playing ball and I recognized a couple of them. Apparently they recognized us as well, for several of them called out "Hello Mrs. Tinsley, hello Rusty", as we lumbered by.

I briefly worried that Rusty might leave the path and join them in their play, and I'm not as steady as I once was on uneven ground. But fortunately he kept to the sidewalk. We passed a young couple sitting on a bench and holding hands. They seemed to be in the middle of a serious conversation, but they stopped to smile at Rusty and nod at me before they returned to their private discussion.

And still Rusty lumbered on, and I lumbered after him.

Two teen-aged girls, sisters perhaps, were going the opposite direction. One of them was holding a leash with a little white poodle at the other end. As they passed by, I heard one say to the other "Look at *her* dog. He just stays right there without running away. I sure wish we could train Topsy to do that."

I smiled to myself. If only they knew that Rusty

was running away. Every now and then my chubby basset would pause and look over his shoulder at me. I understood that he was checking to see if I was still hot on his trail, although I imagine those who saw us just thought it was cute to see the dog looking back to make sure his mistress was still there with him. After all, since we both progressed at the same pace and Rusty had been on his leash until we entered the park, dog and owner were separated by the same distance we would have been had the leash been attached to his collar rather than dangling from my hand.

Truth be told, I'd been enjoying this walk. And I'd been enjoying having someone else in charge for a change. Yes, it might have seemed like we were just following the path, but it was Rusty who decided where we went.

I was starting to wonder when our little journey would end. I was getting a bit tired and we were just barely halfway around the park. We had passed several empty benches, two of which were in the shade, but Rusty didn't give them a second glance. He did pause to sniff at a bench near a bed of irises, but to my disappointment he didn't stop. He continued on his journey, or quest, or whatever it was that we were on.

I'd been distracted by the hopes of stopping to sit on the bench near the irises and when I returned my focus to the path ahead of us I was surprised to see a gentleman approaching. I didn't recognize him. He looked to be around my age. He was wearing gray slacks and a blue polo shirt. His walk was slow but sure, and I was momentarily jealous that he wasn't using a cane. As he got closer, I noticed that he had sparkling green eyes, and a charming smile. And when he was close enough, he bent down to pet Rusty, scratching him behind his right ear. As I approached, he stood up and put out his hand.

"Good afternoon. That's a fine dog you have, although I see he's trying to run away. Would you like some assistance?"

And I realized he was holding his hand out for the leash. Gratefully, I handed it to him and watched him clip it to the ring on Rusty's collar.

"Thank you. Would you care to join us?"

"I'd be delighted," he said. He turned to face the same direction Rusty and I were heading, holding the leash in one hand and holding his other arm out for me to take.

Feeling particularly bold, I said, "I'm Suzanne."

"And I'm Alan."

That was seven years ago. Rusty is no longer with me, of course, but I still think of him each and every time Alan and I go for a walk in the park. I miss Rusty, but overall it has been a wonderful seven years. And to think it all started when my dog ran away.

SILVER LINING

Jonathan Shipley

THE MAIL WAS A disaster. A threatening notice from the bank about my mortgage in arrears and a gloating note from Alicia's lawyer confirming the huge alimony payment they had extorted from me. For a writer barely making ends meet, it was a lot of money.

And then there was a postcard—Peruvian with a Moroccan stamp. No message. Just a big "K" scrawled on the back. Kirk. That surprised a smile from me. Was this notice he was returning home? I could only guess. Appearing out of thin air had always been his style. Kirk walked in strangeness—that's the only way to describe him. But he was always wildly entertaining, and I could use some of that.

I heard a shrill howl. As I turned from the mailbox, elderly Mrs. Mallory waved from her porch next door, a mangy gray tabby pacing the railing beside her. This was a rare event. The old, pathetic excuse for a cat I often saw creeping around the yard and howling miserably, but Mrs. Mallory hardly ever. I waved back. She was a strange, standoffish neighbor in an old, rundown house, but this time she beckoned me across the yard. I went with trepidation. She might be comfortable on a porch with rotting decking and broken railings, but I preferred to live. I halted a couple yards away.

"Such a shame about the mortgage," she called in a hollow, raspy voice.

I felt an instant of culture shock that a housebound neighbor in her eighties knew all about my finances, but that was a small town for you. If the bank was about to foreclose, apparently everyone knew.

"There's always the hidden treasure," she called again. "I've decided to help you find it."

I wasn't amused, not with a big mortgage payment staring at my empty bank account. "I'm not in the mood for jokes, Mrs. Mallory."

"I'm quite serious," she persisted. "Old Mr. Selby had a fortune in Colonial silver with hiding places all over the house—your house. When he passed on, his son nearly took the place apart looking for the silver."

"Did he find it?" I asked, interested in spite of myself.

"Just an empty hidey-hole or two. Several owners have done their share of knocking on walls, but nobody's found anything. Of course, nobody really believes in the treasure these days. It's been too long and everyone who's ever seen it is dead." Her face crinkled into a sad smile. "Or the equivalent thereof."

I stepped forward. "You've seen this mysterious treasure?"

"Once. It was back in the '50s when Old Man Selby invited my mother and me over and served tea in this wonderful old service. Afterward, my mother raved about those pieces. She was sure they were American 18th century. Imagine their value."

I *was* imagining. My expertise was purely *Antiques Roadshow*, but I was guessing upper five figures for a Colonial tea set. Maybe six for genuine Paul Revere. I could pay off the mortgage and finish all the repairs in one fell swoop.

But I was dreaming. People like me didn't find hidden treasure, but—the glimmer of a thought took hold—strange people like Kirk did. And just maybe my superannuated neighbor knew something about the mysterious Kirk.

"Tell me, Mrs. Mallory," I said, coming a little closer despite the ramshackle porch. "I know the Jacksons who sold me the house, but absolutely nothing about any prior owners. Who lived here about fifteen, sixteen years ago?"

She frowned. "The house was vacant a long time before the Jacksons bought it. I don't think anyone was living there fifteen years ago."

I sighed. I should have known the mystery couldn't be solved that easily.

Then she added, "Of course, there was that boy shimmying up the downspout." She began stroking her tabby, almost defensively.

My ears pricked up at not-so-distant memories. The divorce, the move, the kid climbing in a second-story window of my new old house like he owned the place.

"I tried to ignore him," she added, "but right after the lightning strike in your front yard, he started flitting in and out. Cruel to cats, too—turns 'em green." She gave me a sudden, sharp look. "If I help you with the silver, you need to take care of Tabitha. It was a mistake, and she needs the Beacon of Maracaibo to set things right. I'll have no rest until that happens.

Promise me."

"All right," I said hesitantly. I would have asked what I was promising, but she disappeared inside her house, still muttering about green cats.

Whatever I had expected with my Kirk question, it wasn't this. I'd been hoping for a few facts. Almost everything out of Kirk's mouth defied common sense, and now Mrs. Mallory was talking about lightning strikes and green cats.

It didn't make any particular sense that I inherited Kirk when I bought the house, but that's the way it was. He was seldom there—maybe five or six times a year—and more than paid for his room and board in outrageous travel tales. This living mystery could find the silver if anyone could, and he was heading my way from Morocco.

Two days later, I came down to breakfast to find him entrenched in the kitchen with a bowl of cereal. He looked like a perfectly normal college kid chewing away, not at all mysterious. I wasn't fooled for a moment. At his feet, Mrs. Mallory's sickly tabby lapped weakly at a bowl of milk. "Why did you bring the cat inside?" I asked.

"Didn't," he mumbled. "Already here when I arrived. Thought you adopted the poor old thing."

Had I left the door open? "So, green cats," I said, sitting down across from him. First cats, then silver.

"It did *not* happen as reported by Old Lady Mallory," he sputtered, mouth full of Cheerios. He chewed, swallowed, and continued more clearly. "It was an accident. I never meant to turn her cat green."

This was only going to get worse. "You turned her cat green by accident?"

"Completely," he nodded, then pushed his mop of

13

brown hair out of his eyes. "I was spray painting the grass and never even saw the damn cat."

I continued to bite. "And why were you painting the grass?"

"It had been a dry summer, the kind where the grass turns brown if you don't water every five minutes. Well, it was Turner's job to water—he was the Jacksons' son. But there were these brown stripes across the lawn where he'd missed some places. And with his parents coming home just before the Garden Club competition—well, you get the picture."

Sort of. "The son wasn't doing his job, so you painted the grass to cover for him. Did it ever occur to you he might learn more by facing the consequences of his negligence?"

Kirk rolled his eyes. "Turner wasn't negligent. He was trying really hard. He just couldn't tell the difference."

"Between dead grass and healthy grass?" Even *I* could tell that.

"He was color-blind. Brown and green looked the same to him. And even the cat part wasn't so bad in the long run. Old Lady Mallory would never admit it, but this here cat became famous—"

"Stop." If I listened to any more, I was going to end up with a headache. "New topic—Old Man Selby's silver."

His eyes lit up like blue light bulbs. "Great story, huh? And no one's ever claimed it. Sort of like having a Spanish galleon floating around the basement."

I'd learned to sift Kirk's words with extraordinary care. "No one's ever *claimed* it or no one's ever *found* it?"

He gave me a roguish grin. "No, *I* haven't found it.

14

Sure, I've looked, but Old Man Selby was a real paranoid."

"So I've heard. But the bank is about to foreclose on the house, and I really need a little treasure in my life right now. So where do I start looking? Upstairs, downstairs, or attic?"

"Upstairs, maybe?" He went back to his cereal, looking unusually thoughtful as he chewed.

I knew the signs. Kirk was a good liar, one of the best in creation. But listening to his tales had sensitized me to certain clues. Something in his facial expression when he said "upstairs" set off fiction alarms. He knew more than he was telling me.

I left him in the kitchen and went off to read the mail because I was starting to feel very uncomfortable. I knew how easily money could come between people. Seeing my wife of ten years suddenly turn into the Greed Queen was not a pleasant memory. I hated the thought of seeing that in Kirk, who had always seemed immune to material goods.

I set my suspicions aside, but the next evening they came back full force. On my way downstairs, I felt a rumble run through the steps beneath my feet. The only thing under the stairs was an empty coat closet. I crouched down, listening to the shuffling, wondering what he was doing down there. Then the closet rumbled again, and through the banister I saw Kirk heading for the outside door. Something gleamed in his hand as he passed by the lamp... something silver.

The moment he disappeared, I rushed downstairs and began tapping the woodwork in the closet. A small wooden bump yielded under my fingertips and the whole back wall slid into a wall pocket with a rumble. The compartment behind it wasn't large, just four shallow shelves. But each shelf was heaped with silver. Well, not heaped. As far as hidden treasures went, there was less than I expected. I counted about two dozen items, mostly candlesticks and heavily engraved plates. But no tea set.

Suspicions surfaced. Ugly suspicions. Kirk had to be funding his travels somehow, and he had no visible income. I closed up the closet and hurried outside. I could just see Kirk two blocks down turning the corner onto Maple Avenue. I went after him, guessing he was heading for the all-night pawn shop on Maple. When I reached the shop, I walked slowly past the window and saw a silver candlestick changing hands.

The walk home depressed me. It wasn't the lie per se. Part of Kirk's charm was his ability to mix wonderful lies into any incident. But his lies had always been entertaining, not deceitful. This was different. He had found the treasure—and I granted that could have happened years before I entered the picture. But not to come clean when I asked? He knew I needed the money.

I felt an old familiar feeling. Sold out.

Maybe Kirk had his reasons, maybe Alicia had her reasons. But dammit, I had reasons too. This time I refused to roll over and give up.

***

The next morning I loaded all the hidden silver into a cardboard carton and headed for a jewelry store on Henderson Avenue. I walked into the shop and asked the proprietor to take a look.

The moment he opened the box and started turning over items to check the marks, a terrible doubt came over me. "Uh, this isn't silverplate, is it?"

The jeweler shook his head without looking up. "Definitely not... mostly coin silver and 800 silver."

I was lost. "What does that mean?"

"It's solid silver, but with different percentages of silver to copper. Virtually nothing is 100% pure silver because it's so soft."

"But it could be American—old American," I persisted.

He shrugged. "Off the top of my head, I can't tell you anything much. But yes, probably old. I'll look up the hallmarks and have answers for you tomorrow."

I headed home, playing the good and bad in my head. Having money again was good. Maybe even lots of money. But what to do about Kirk. I'd been stupid—that's all there was to it. I'd let a complete stranger into my house and actually trusted him for the sole reason that he was interesting. Phrased like that, it seemed like more than stupidity. More like mentally challenged. Alicia and money and betrayal all over again, just on a smaller scale. The world is cruel; people are cruel. You'd think I would have learned the first time.

By the time I arrived home, I was well into divorce court mentality. Numb the emotions, say what needs to be said, and get that person out of your life as quickly as possible.

I found Kirk in the stair hall, looking unsettled. "I think we've been burgled," he said when he saw me. "Look at this—"

"I know about your secret closet. I have the silver. I don't care how much of Old Man Selby's treasure you've taken in the past, I just want you gone. I don't want to discuss it. Just go and don't come back."

His face underwent some extraordinary changes

before settling into an expression of tense enlightenment. "Oh, you think—"

I didn't *think*, I *knew*. "I don't want to discuss it," I repeated. "Just go and don't come back."

Considering how miserable I was, I did a good job of being unfeeling and unyielding. Divorce court had taught me well.

Kirk looked bewildered. "But—"

"Go. Don't be here when I get back." I turned and left.

I hadn't made the end of the block before my hands starting shaking. The numbness was wearing off. My mind slipped into its usual, wishy-washy mode. What if I was wrong? Maybe I'd misinterpreted.

I hoped that Kirk took me seriously and left. If he was still there, I would be apologizing all over myself, trying to patch things up. I kept walking. It was twilight before I returned home. The house loomed dark and empty, and I nearly tripped over Mrs. Mallory's skeletal tabby curled up unexpectedly at the front door. It yowled and skittered off, which didn't improve my nerves any. I took a deep breath and went up to Kirk's bedroom. No telltale duffle bag. The closet stood open and empty.

Good, I told myself. I felt miserable.

***

The jeweler greeted me with a big smile the next morning. "I have those answers for you."

"So this is really Old Man Selby's treasure?"

His expression dissolved into surprise. "That old yarn? No, no connection at all. None of these pieces are anywhere near old enough."

"You said it was old," I insisted. This *had* to be the treasure.

"Well, yes. But I was thinking 1940s. Most people think anything over half a century is old."

A feeling of failure descended like a black drape. "So are these things worth anything?"

He nodded. "Certainly. It's mostly 800 silver, probably six to eight thousand dollars' worth altogether. But none of it is particularly rare. Just unusual in this country."

"This country?" I asked guardedly.

"Yes, the 800 stuff is Latin American, probably Peruvian. The coin silver pieces seem to be Moroccan."

Peru. Morocco. Who did I know that traveled in those regions? My stomach knotted. I had confiscated the Kirk equivalent of a savings account.

"Are you still thinking of selling?" the jeweler asked after a long silence. "I'll give you a fair price."

The bank foreclosure seemed suddenly distant and unimportant. I shook my head and picked up the heavy carton.

After a week, I realized Kirk had taken me at my word and really was gone. A strange sense of aloneness settled over me. Oddly enough, Mrs. Mallory's pathetic old cat that had never flicked a whisker at me before suddenly staked out the front door as its own. Cat—green cat—Kirk. It was oddly comforting in a masochistic way. I started feeding it, even though it kept sneaking inside the house when I wasn't looking.

The bank wasn't very receptive to refinancing the mortgage, but I figured I could wear them down before I hit the critical mark. The situation was completely ludicrous. Yes, I'd jumped to a wrong conclusion to everyone's grief. And now here I was, performing an empty act of honor that no one would ever appreciate. Common sense said sell the Peruvian silver and try to make it up to Kirk later if and when I saw him again. But I couldn't do it.

I pawned everything else—my ultra-HD camera, my watch, my big-screen TV. A few hundred dollars against the mega-thousands I owed. But enough to make a good faith payment, I hoped. Then one afternoon when the guilt was especially bad, the inevitable happened. I tripped over the tabby that had once again gotten inside in some strange cat way. As I sat massaging a scraped shin, the seed of an idea took root. An immature, outrageous, and totally indefensible idea. Or maybe I would think of a defense by the time Mrs. Mallory descended on me in all her wrath. But it didn't matter. I had to try.

***

Within the hour the doorbell rang. The sight of Kirk who came and went like a ghost, standing and waiting for permission to enter tore at me. The whole mystery of his being seemed diminished.

"It was inexcusable on my part," I began. "I was hoping to see you again to make proper apologies—and of course, return your property to you. I would invite you to take up residence again, but I know that breaking faith with someone sours the relationship forever. I've been there—I actually loved my wife once upon a time, you know."

Kirk just stood there waiting until I wound down, then said, "It was a mistake, not the end of the world. I just wasn't sure if you knew the score. But when I saw your message"—he glanced pointedly at Mrs.

Mallory's cat—"well, it doesn't take a genius. Can I come in?"

The intensity of the moment had obscured the fact that we were still on the stoop, the old tabby curling around our legs—a tabby now sporting a fresh coat of neon-green paint. Extreme, but it had worked. Shooing the cat off the porch, I led Kirk into the dining room. "Your silver is in the carton under the table. If you want to check the contents—"

Kirk gave a snort. "Hey, I'm not the one who went through divorce hell. I still trust people."

Point taken.

"But," he continued, "I *am* the one you can't get rid of because I come with the house."

It sure sounded like a second chance and did a lot for the guilt complex I'd been hauling around. But at this stage, it didn't really make a difference.

"Then it looks like you'll be going with the house as well." I shrugged. "Maybe you'll have better luck with the next owner."

Kirk's face quirked into a sour expression. "Don't even think it. Do you have any idea how hard it is to train new owners? I'm not ready to change again. I give you the silver. All of it."

I shook my head firmly. "I'd rather be evicted with honor."

"*Evictus cum laude*," he intoned solemnly. "Sounds pretty lame when the bank is about to foreclose. Take the stuff and cash it in, and we'll both be happy."

He really meant it. Not a polite gesture, not even a sacrificial gesture. Material assets meant nothing to him. Maybe there were a lot of Alicias in the world, but Kirk wasn't one of them.

"I wasn't holding out about the secret closet and the silver—not really," he added. "It was just out of sight, out of mind. But when you brought up Old Man Selby, I got this crazy idea to sell it and surprise you with a mortgage payment. It's probably not enough but... surprise!"

A gift. A universe away from everything I'd been thinking. I felt I should apologize again. Unfortunately, he was right—his Moroccan silver wasn't enough to save the house. I cleared my throat. Suddenly the green tabby was twining around my feet, rubbing paint flecks onto my pant legs. And this time I was sure I hadn't let him in. "That cat is starting to take after you," I told Kirk. "It's been coming and going like a ghost."

"Guess it's lonely." He gave the cat a long, thoughtful look, one ghost to another, as it were. "When I was seriously searching the place years ago, I found a bunch more secret cupboards and bolt holes besides the one under the stairs—all empty, of course. Maybe kitty here found one I missed. Maybe even the jackpot."

That galvanized me to action. "And it has to be close by since the cat was on the porch a second ago." I began scrutinizing the woodwork. Nothing near the front door, but the couch in the living room sported telltale flecks of green on its dust ruffle. I stepped in that direction, Kirk right behind me.

"There." He pointed to the fireplace where another trace of green showed at the base of the mantel. "And that's the fireplace that has never worked."

"Bricked-up flue." I nodded. "Why anyone would brick up a chimney opening I can't imagine—"

As soon as I uttered the words, the answer stared me in the face: to keep anyone from building a fire there... because fire would damage the silver. A second later, I was down on my knees, pulling out the old brass andirons and fireback. A small iron door stood half open. I'd seen it before, though never open. It was a disposal chute for ashes, or so the realtor had said. But I had never given a thought to where the ash chute led. Outside, obviously, but I'd never checked. Apparently the cat had.

I pulled the ash door fully open and stuck a hand inside. The bottom and sides were lined with metal, but the top of the chute was strangely nonexistent. A moment later, my probing fingers encountered a ledge and came into contact with... something.

"What?" Kirk prompted, clued in by my frozen expression.

"There's something up above the chute to the right," I murmured. "But I can't quite angle my hand to get hold of it."

"Let me," he offered. "When I was traveling with the circus, I hung with a contortionist who taught me how to—"

"Stop," I ordered, giving up my place on the hearth. "No stories—just do it."

A moment later, three lumpy masses of newspaper were sitting on the floor between us. The newsprint was brittle and yellow but still legible. I spotted "May 12, 1951" and my heartbeat went into high gear. Mrs. Mallory's tea party.

I carefully removed the layers of newspaper on the first lump until a lidless sugar bowl emerged. Very tarnished but very silver. I just sat there, unable to do anything but stare. I couldn't quite let myself believe we had found the treasure. The other lumps were undoubtedly the teapot and creamer. "Paul Revere?" I whispered.

Kirk reached down and lifted the sugar bowl, rubbing the bottom with his thumb to cut through the tarnish. "Myer Myers," he said, squinting at the hallmark that appeared under his thumb. "Cool."

"Who?"

"Myer Myers, colonial silversmith from New York. Probably worth as much as Revere."

I accepted that as fact, just because Kirk was Kirk. But I still had to ask. "Why are you so much into silver? Gold holds its value better."

He shook his head. "Ever tried transporting gold? Customs gets in a real snit about bringing undeclared gold into the country."

"But silver's the same problem," I argued. "Metal detectors, airport security, customs."

He shook his head violently. "No, that's the beauty of it. Silver—solid silver, at least—doesn't set off the metal detectors. I can sneak it right through."

"Silver doesn't set off the metal detectors?" I repeated dubiously. "You expect me to believe that?"

"Sure, it's the mystical properties of silver that make it behave differently than other metals. An old shaman in Peru clued me in."

"An old shaman?" I scoffed. "Mystical properties? You lie like a lawyer."

"At times." he shrugged. "But not about something like this. It was up in this mountain village and this old guy pulls me aside to warn me about smugglers looting the ruins..."

I sat there, basking in the story. We'd found the treasure, the house was saved, and our relationship seemed to be back together like some miraculous Humpty Dumpty. For the moment, all was right with the world.

I needed to hang onto that thought when I faced Mrs. Mallory tomorrow. Right on cue, the mangy, neon-green tabby stuck her face in the teapot, howling urgently. I sighed. "Mrs. Mallory is not going to be pleased when next we talk."

Kirk gave me the oddest look. "So the two of you... talk?"

"Not often. But now I have the cat to explain, plus I need to thank her. She's the one who told me about the Selby silver—even said she'd help me find it. Maybe we should all have a celebratory tea party before the silver goes to Sotheby's."

Kirk's eyes just kept getting bigger as I talked.

"What?" I demanded.

He took a deep breath. "Old Lady Mallory died years before you moved in. Her house has been bound up in estate purgatory, which is why it's sitting there empty and derelict."

"But she had a conversation with me," I insisted. "She called me over and told me about the silver."

He shifted uneasily. "Did you make any sort of deal with her? Promise her your firstborn or anything in exchange for the silver?"

Suddenly the afternoon felt cold and dark. "There was a promise involved," I said slowly. "It was something like—"

"Word for word," Kirk interrupted. "When you make deals with the dead, every syllable is important."

I wasn't sure why I believed any of this, but I recalled Mrs. Mallory's comment about everyone who had ever seen the silver being dead... or the equivalent thereof—oddly ambiguous phrasing that made more sense now. I should have noticed—as in no mail, no electricity, ramshackle porch—that the house next door was much too derelict to support life. I carefully reconstructed my conversation with Mrs. Mallory to reclaim the exact words: *"If I help you with the silver, you need to take care of Tabitha. It was a mistake, and she needs the Beacon of Maracaibo to set things right. I'll have no rest until that happens. Promise me.* That's what she said."

Kirk mulled the words for a long moment. "Sounds OK—not like a killer ghost trying to suck out your soul."

"Mrs. Mallory?"

"You haven't seen the dark side of the old crow. But it sounds like she is trying to move on, just can't. Not while kitty is in limbo."

"So she wants me to adopt her cat and take care of it." I nodded. That sounded easy.

He shook his head. "No. Think about the other meaning—eh, bambino, you need to *take care of* a little problem for la familia. It's the curse."

I blinked. "What now?"

"Kitty's really old, you have to understand—older than me. But Old Lady Mallory loved her cat and didn't want it dying on her, so she had one of her witchy friends do a spell—she knew people like that. Then she died suddenly and kitty's a hundred years old in cat years but can't die because it's been cursed to keep living. And look at it—miserable. That's the mistake she wants to fix."

"Oh." And suddenly I was cast as a cat killer. "But I refuse to bash in its head or anything like that."

"One would hope," Kirk snorted. "I hate sharing space with head-bashers. And that's not what she said anyway. The Beacon of Maracaibo is on the Catatumbo

River in Venezuela—lightning capital of the world—thousands of strikes every hour. All sorts of local myths about it being the Gate of Life and Death. So I'm guessing Beacon trumps spell, and kitty can die there."

Suddenly a trip to Venezuela, but I wasn't complaining with a treasure trove at my feet. There'd be complications—cat on an airplane, especially an old, sick cat. You'd think a quick trip to the vet would get the same result, but that wasn't the promise.

Kirk leaned in. "You know, I really ought to come along, this being more my neck of the woods and all."

"But it's my task, not yours," I pointed out. "I gave the promise."

"And I'm offering to help," Kirk responded. "As an apology, if nothing else. I mean, think about it. I probably should make amends to Old Lady Mallory for all that green cat stuff. Speaking from experience, there's nothing worse than a ghost with a grudge..."

And we were off again on a wild story, which at that moment seemed perfectly rational and not at all outrageous. Maybe it all had to do with the scale of weirdness. After a dead next-door neighbor and a hundred-year-old cat, a story from a mysterious kid who crawled through second-floor windows was normal as apple pie. But he was right—this was his tale as well as mine.

"OK, we both go to Venezuela," I said abruptly in the middle of his ghost story. "But no weirdness from you."

He considered a moment with cocked head, then grinned. "Well, I can't promise but—"

"No, no 'buts'," I said firmly. "I do *not* want to end up in one of your crazy adventures."

Or maybe that ship had already sailed.

PATIENCE

R. J. Meldrum

IT WAS A BRIGHT, BEAUTIFUL summer's day. That morning, Mequillen and his team had driven up from London to the northern part of Norfolk. There were three of them, himself, Don, and Jackie. They worked for a television production company. The trio worked well together and they were good at their jobs, which on this particular occasion was to find the perfect location for a television series set in the 1950s. They were scouting out the old army and R.A.F. bases scattered around the county. First on their list was R.A.F. Highmoor.

Highmoor was an excellent candidate for the shoot. Built in 1938, it was a collection of brick and concrete buildings and prefabricated metal hangars arranged in seemingly chaotic order next to a tarmacked runway. Rotting window frames, broken windows, and walls smeared with graffiti greeted the team. A derelict control tower, its windows shattered, sat mournfully gazing over the abandoned site. Highmoor had been used as a base for Lancaster bombers between 1942 and 1944. It had been abandoned for good in 1947.

Mequillen directed the others to take some photographs of the buildings, while he wandered further afield to take some measurements, planning to plot out some likely camera angles. He walked to the edge of the runway, looking at the crumbling tarmac. His grandfather had fought in the Second World War and Mequillen remembered that the old man would sometimes show off the shrapnel wounds on his leg that he had acquired in North Africa. Must have been tough to have to fight, to kill. Mequillen could only imagine what it would have been like to be in your early twenties, climbing into a Lancaster bomber and flying off into the blue sky to drop bombs onto German cities. So many of them had never come home. Mequillen had done some background reading on the bases and the airmen; the attrition rate amongst bomber flight crews had been horrendous.

He shook his head slightly, focusing once more on the job in hand. Glancing around, he noticed something strange. There was a small white dog sitting at the edge of the derelict runway, about fifty feet away. It was staring down the runway, towards the east where the bombers would have come in to land, its tail wagging at a slow pace. It made for an odd sight. Mequillen, wondering if it was lost, decided to head towards it. As he got nearer, within ten feet or so, the dog noticed his presence and darted away, running between two of the nearby metal huts. Mequillen didn't chase it, knowing full well that a dog that didn't want to be caught would never be caught. He turned back to meet up with the others.

The team had opted to stay overnight in a local pub in a nearby village. There were a couple of other locations to check out in the general area before they headed back to London the next evening. As they ate their evening meal in the thatched pub, Mequillen found that his mind was still focused on the dog he had seen. It was a distinct possibility that the little dog was lost. Why else would it be hanging around an abandoned airbase? He decided to ask the barman. It was a pretty small village and he might know if a local dog had gone missing. Mequillen could never have anticipated the response he got. The barman just smiled and laughed.

"Not a lost dog, not as such. That'll be old Tommy that you saw. Little white dog, right?"

"Yes, that's right. A little white dog."

"He's not lost. He's been at the old base for over seventy years now, always in the same spot. Waiting for 'is master to return from the war."

Mequillen gaped at the man, his face flushing with anger.

"That's not funny you know. I was only concerned about the wee dog."

The barman laughed again and turned to serve the next customer.

"He isn't joking, you know," said a well-dressed man sitting at the bar, sipping Scotch. He leant over, extending his hand. They shook hands.

"Dr. Williams, local G.P."

"Dan Mequillen. I work for Source Productions down in London. We're up here scouting locations. Highmoor could be good as the location for a forthcoming television series. That's where I saw this mysterious dog."

Williams smiled.

"The tale is true you know. I didn't believe it

myself when I first arrived in the area, but it really is true. Tommy was the dog's name. The story is that he belonged to a Lancaster pilot and Tommy always waited for him at the edge of the runway when his master was away on a mission. One day in 1942 his master didn't come back, but Tommy kept waiting. And waiting. Tommy died in 1946, just before the base closed for good, but his ghost remains there, waiting for the sound of the engines; the sound that signals his master is returning. But his master didn't return that one night in 1942, nor will he ever return. I guess Tommy will be there forever."

"Surely you don't believe this? You, a doctor?"

"I do, Mr. Mequillen. I really do."

Williams seemed serious and sincere, but Mequillen simply didn't believe him. He suspected that the two locals were teasing him and dismissed their fanciful tales. But there was still the issue of the lost dog. It looked as if he would have to do something about it himself, since no one in the village seemed willing to help.

The next morning Mequillen sent his colleagues along to the next location without him, while he returned to the airbase. He wanted to see if the dog was still there and to see if, this time, he could get hold of it. He wanted to find out if it had tags or a microchip, so that it could be returned to its rightful owner.

Parking at the airbase, he exited the car and headed back to where he had stood the day before. Looking down the edge of the runway, he saw that the dog was sitting in the same spot. And, as before, the dog was gazing down the runway, almost as if he was waiting for a plane to return. Shaking his head in disgust at himself for being so suggestible, Mequillen walked towards the dog, but once more it noticed his presence and took off running between the buildings and out of sight. This time Mequillen chased him. Rounding the corner of one of the buildings, Mequillen experienced one of the most amazing sights of his entire life. He saw that the little white dog was running between two metal buildings, about twenty feet ahead of him. The dog headed towards a brick wall that blocked his escape route. But, as the dog approached the wall he didn't slow down or try to avoid it. Instead he went straight through, as if the solid, red brick barrier simply wasn't there.

Mequillen gasped in amazement and stopped dead. It was suddenly true. This wasn't a lost dog. This was a ghost. An urge came to him. He needed to find out more about this dog from seventy years ago. He went to see Dr. Williams.

Williams wasn't surprised to see Mequillen, in fact he was rather pleased. Mequillen looked embarrassed, but described what he had seen. Williams smiled.

"You've experienced what many of us have. Tommy always follows that same route. Between the two metal buildings and then through the solid brick wall. That's why he can't be caught."

Mequillen then asked the question he felt he needed to ask. In response, Williams told Mequillen that there was only one village resident who could possibly help him. Cockerlyne. Williams told him that Cockerlyne was ninety-two years old and had been stationed at Highmoor during the war. After the armistice he had married a local girl and settled in the area. He still lived in the village, looked after by a small army of nurses and caregivers. Mequillen thanked the doctor and went on his way. He called on Cockerlyne that afternoon. He found the old man sitting on his front porch.

Introducing himself, he asked his question. "Mr. Cockerlyne, I'm interested in finding out about Tommy, the little dog who sits on the runway at Highmoor. Please tell me his story."

Cockerlyne grunted.

"Heard the tales, have you lad? You've seen him too, I'll wager. You're not the first to come and ask me. Many people have tried to catch him, but how can you catch a ghost? Especially one that runs as fast as he does through solid walls!"

The old man laughed at his own joke.

"The dog you saw *is* the ghost of little Tommy. I remember Tommy, remember him well from the war. I wasn't flight crew, I was ground crew loading the bombs and I remember the little fellow sitting at the edge of the runway every time they went on a mission. I remember, clear as day, the time they didn't come back. Hamburg it was. Out of twenty bombers that left the base, only five made it back. The flak got some of them, the fighters got the rest. Some went down over the city, others over the sea on the way home. His master was one of them that got lost. After that, Tommy just sat there day after day; we tried to get him to move, rehome him even, but he wouldn't shift. Died in that very spot in '46. We buried him right there too. The Group Captain said not to, but who cared about him, the war was over and I was being discharged the next month."

For Mequillen, there was suddenly another question he needed to ask. An important question. Some instinct told him that it might be the most important question.

"Mr. Cockerlyne, what was the name of Tommy's owner? The pilot of that Lancaster."

Cockerlyne closed his eyes and lay back in his chair. For a few moments, Mequillen thought he'd gone to sleep, but then he spoke.

"Flight-Lieutenant Peter Winston. A nice lad, only young. Not one of the pompous, arrogant ones. He was ordinary, working class, not like those posh blokes. A good pilot by all accounts too. But when there's flak and fighters, even the best pilots can die. Not much that skill can do when you're flying straight on the bomb run. His plane was called Lucky Lucy after his girl back home. Lucky Lucy went down over Hamburg, shredded by flak. A night raid, taking off at dusk and returning at dawn. Those Germans had some very accurate flak. Just lads themselves too, defending their city. The boys who saw the Lucky Lucy go down said they saw no parachutes; likely the lads were already dead, or at least too injured to jump."

The old man shook his head. "Horrible way to go. Horrible."

Mequillen said, "Thank you Mr. Cockerlyne, thank you very much."

Mequillen had a feeling that he knew what he had to do. He would have to wait until the next day.

The next morning, he made sure that he was at Highmoor just before dawn, the same time that the bombers would have returned from their night raids. He saw that Tommy was still waiting in his appointed spot, still gazing hopefully into the eastern sky. There was finally no doubt in his mind that the story was true. Day after day, night after night Tommy waited for his master to return, not even death could stop him. Mequillen hoped that his plan would work and that

Tommy would find peace. He walked towards the dog, speaking softly.

"Tommy, Tommy, Tommy," he sang the name of the dog. "You've been waiting so long for him, haven't you? Waiting for Peter to come home."

This time the dog did not move. Instead his ears pricked up at the sound of his master's name.

"You know what, Tommy. I think I know why you've had to wait for so long. You've needed something that no one realised. Something you can't do yourself. They are lost out there somewhere and they need someone to call them home. To bring the Lucky Lucy back."

Tommy didn't move. Mequillen turned to the runway, looking eastward into the sun that was starting to peek over the horizon. He closed his eyes and spoke.

"Lucky Lucy, Lucky Lucy, Lucky Lucy. Come home, you've been away too long. Peter Winston, Peter Winston, Peter Winston, come home. Tommy is waiting for you."

He stopped speaking and waited. There was a sound in the distance. An engine. He couldn't see properly, the light from the rising sun was making him squint and there was a haze on the runway, but he was sure it was the noise of a propeller-driven plane. Unable to see it, all he could do was listen. The noise of the engines got louder and louder, and then there was a sudden squeal of tires on tarmac as the unseen plane landed. Mequillen heard the plane taxi briefly then come to a halt. The engines shut down. He looked down at Tommy. He was still there, sitting on the edge of the tarmac, his tail wagging furiously. Mequillen knew that he would have been trained to stay put; runways were dangerous places. Voices sounded from the tarmac, but

Mequillen couldn't see anything in the hazy early morning sunshine.

"Good flight, lads. That'll show those Krauts. Same again tomorrow!"

There was laughter.

"Now, where's the little fellow? Where's my Tommy?"

Mequillen looked down at the dog and Tommy finally met his gaze. His tail flicked in anticipation.

"Go to him," said Mequillen. Tommy went. Mequillen watched as the small white dog raced ecstatically across the tarmac towards the unseen figures. The last thing Mequillen saw was the enthusiastically wagging tail as Tommy disappeared into the sunny haze of the dawn. Mequillen heard delighted squeals and barks from Tommy and more laughter from the crew, but the noises were fading now. Soon, they faded away completely and Mequillen found himself alone on the edge of the runway of a disused airbase in Norfolk, with the sun slowly rising in the east.

ADOPTING CATHY

Ginny Swart

WHEN I WAS GROWING UP, my mother gave me an excellent piece of advice concerning adoption.

"Choose one with a kind voice and gentle hands," she said. "And if she has a little garden, so much the better."

So when I heard Cathy Burnett talking to the baker one morning, I stopped trying to catch a grasshopper, peered around the boxes on the pavement and took a critical look.

Short fair hair, big brown eyes, and a wide smile that seemed to include me. That was a good start. I crept a little closer.

"Is this your kitten, Mr. Harris?"

Before I knew it, she'd scooped me up and cuddled me against her neck, stroking me softly. Heaven! Even though I wanted to appear cool, I started purring immediately, I just couldn't help myself.

"That? No, it's a stray. Been hanging around here for few days. Doesn't seem to belong to anyone."

Well! Excuse me! *Belong* to someone? Did the poor man seriously think that cats *belong* to people?

Cathy held me away from her and looked into my eyes.

"He's so unusual, these dark blue eyes and cream fur with darker stripes."

"Got a touch of Siamese if you ask me. They can be noisy, Siamese can. Very demanding."

"He's gorgeous. If he really doesn't belong to anyone…would you like to come home and live with me, kitty?"

And that is how I came to adopt Cathy.

"I think I'll call you Baker," she said on the way home. "Seeing that's where we met."

Mmm. I'd have preferred a name with a touch more class, like Hamlet or Shalimar but I decided to go with what she chose.

Cathy was very well-behaved from the start. She knew cats like to be fed twice a day and bought me the right sized feeding bowl and some special cat food that tasted rather nice. No more chasing around after grasshoppers and mice and worrying about where my next meal was coming from, then!

And I had my own little basket lined with an old cushion, right at Cathy's feet next to her armchair.

But the best thing was, she lived in a ground floor flat. So I had a garden of my own, and once her brother Tom had fitted a clever little opening at the bottom of the kitchen door especially for me, I could come in and out as I liked.

"How's it going, Cath?" he asked, once he'd fitted the door and she'd made him a cup of tea. "Are you handling things okay?"

"I'm fine."

Did he mean me? Was he worried that I was making too many demands on his sister? Surely not!

"I heard he's gone off to London and joined some big company there."

Not me then.

"Good riddance, I say. If he ever comes back here he'll have me to deal with."

"Don't, Tom." Cathy patted his hand. "I'm fine. It's over. Lance is history and I'm moving on, I promise."

"Glad to hear it. You've found yourself a nice friendly cat, haven't you? Got a purr like a tractor starting up!"

I could always tell when someone's a cat-lover, and Tom had a good wide lap, but when he made the ridiculous mistake about ownership, I was forced to jump down and walk off in disapproval with my tail held high.

I stayed out until he'd gone. Then I heard Cathy calling me.

"Baker! Baker! Time for our programme!"

And I dashed inside with as much dignity as I could, using my new cat-flap. Which was a great improvement on calling her to open the door for me each time. A fast learner in many ways, Cathy is.

Don't ask me how I became hooked on *Eastenders.* I suppose it was because Cathy watched it every day herself, and I'd sit on her lap and we'd enjoy it together while she had a cup of tea and stroked me in her special way.

I could never quite work out what was going on. There were too many people, all arguing and making-up and gossiping about each other. But we never missed an episode, although in my experience, real life wasn't a bit like that, not in Cathy's flat at any rate. Things were very quiet.

I worried a bit about my Cathy. She didn't seem to have any fun and she hardly ever went out except with her friend Amy. It wasn't right that someone so young and pretty should watch TV alone every night and I wished I could help her find the right mate.

The two girls went to the pictures and sometimes Amy would come back for cocoa and they'd sit and talk. About men, mostly. About how awful they were and how happy they both were, not to have one in their lives.

Hey, I said, you've got *me!* But even rubbing my head against Cathy's hand and purring fit to bust didn't seem to take that sad look from her eyes when she talked about Lance.

"I used to think we were forever, you know what I mean?" she said softly. "Then he left me that note... I don't think I'll ever trust a man again. I really thought I knew him but look how wrong I was."

"Don't tell me! You never met Mike, but he was just the same, made all sorts of promises then off he went to America and never came back. He never even wrote to me. After we'd chosen the ring and everything. Not that he'd ever bought it, like he said he would. I'm off men forever, Cath, that's for sure."

"Me too. Who needs them? Have some more cocoa."

But she didn't mean that, I could tell. Cats know these things and I could sense her loneliness.

So you can imagine how pleased I was when she brought Rob back for my approval. She spent all afternoon making something that smelled delicious with cheese and mushrooms and little bits and pieces. Not that I'm mad about mushrooms but I know she likes them.

40

I may as well mention that Cathy had one small fault, but then, nobody's perfect. She's a vegetarian. So boring! I hardly ever got any tasty tidbits. I mean, who wants leftover broccoli? But I'm not complaining. I can always catch a mouse for variety, although I'm ashamed to admit I'd become awfully lazy about finding my own food. Having a person at your beck and call does that to a cat.

Once the meal was made she changed into a pretty blue dress I hadn't seen before and lit some candles.

"Now what music do you think he'd like, Baker?" she murmured, but I know a rhetorical question when I hear one. She put on something with violins, my favourite instrument, and started waltzing around the room all by herself and I could feel the happy vibrations from where I sat.

But the minute he came through the door, I had my doubts about Rob. Deep voice, nice smile, and a big bunch of red roses in his hand but there was something about him that just wasn't right.

"Nice place you have here, Cathy," he said, handing over the flowers. "Ah, I see you're a cat person." He bent down and snapped his fingers. "Here, kitty kitty!"

Of course I ignored him and he straightened up, laughing. "I prefer dogs, myself," he said. "Actually, cats give me hay fever."

"Oh dear, maybe I should put Baker outside then," she said, doubtfully.

Well, I didn't want to cause a scene so I walked out as if I'd thought of it first, but I could hear perfectly well from the kitchen. And I didn't like what I heard.

Rob was totally a "me" person. Everything was about himself. How smart he was at work, how well he played sport, the kind of films he liked to see, his opinion on just about everything. I could hear Cathy saying things like "Oh, I see," and "Is that so?" but she didn't sound very impressed. I sensed her disappointment.

Ho hum, I thought, we missed *Eastenders* for *this?* I wished he'd go.

Then I heard her say, "No, Rob, I'd rather you didn't do that," and pretty soon, in an odd sort of voice, "Rob! Will you stop that, please!"

I hurried through to the sitting room and there he was sitting much too close to Cathy, who was red in the face, and I could tell she was upset.

Well, I'm not an idiot, I knew I couldn't scratch him effectively through his thick socks, so I went for the subtle approach.

I jumped upon his lap and started to talk loudly, pushing my face against his and pretending I thought he was wonderful.

"Get this wretched animal off me," he said shortly, trying to shove me away. "And what a racket it's making, like a baby yowling. I can't stand cats. They make me... a-woo-shoo! A-woo-shoo!"

"Oh, but Baker's taken a fancy to you," said Cathy, and she smiled wickedly. "Haven't you, Baker?"

"A-woo-shoo! A-woo-shoo!"

I leaned closer and patted his face with my paw, forgetting to retract my claws. Silly me.

"Ouch! I'm bleeding!"

Eyes streaming and dabbing his cheek, Rob left soon afterwards, slamming the door. We could hear him sneezing all the way to his car.

"He didn't even want to stay for coffee!" Cathy giggled as she told Amy the story of her disastrous date.

"Baker rescued me from an idiot that just didn't want to take no for an answer. You're the smartest cat in the world, aren't you, my beautiful boy?"

Who was I to disagree?

After that there were more film evenings with Amy and life settled into a pleasant if dull routine.

Then everything changed.

I was sitting on the wall waiting for Cathy to come home when a man walked past carrying something that smelled absolutely marvelous. I'd never known anything like it before. It was magnet, that canvas knapsack, and I followed as closely as I could until he went into a house three doors down, and closed the front door.

So it had to be the tradesman's entrance. I'm not proud. His house was exactly like Cathy's and I jumped up onto the kitchen window sill and stepped inside.

"Smelled the fish, did you, kitty?"

I sensed an instant affiliation between us. He had deep blue eyes, very like my own and a nice smile. He was cutting up something and he handed me a piece to taste.

"Like fish, do you?"

Heaven! So this was what fish tasted like. And there was more where that came from! His whole bag was full of the silver-grey things, all smelling wonderful. I started to purr encouragingly and he laughed, stroking me under the chin and feeding me more little bits.

"You're no stray," he said. "Too well fed for that. But you certainly like fish, don't you?"

I couldn't help agreeing.

I watched as he cleaned the other fish and put them in his freezer and I noticed a whole lot more there already.

"That's the problem with fishing as a hobby," he told me seriously. "I can't eat them fast enough all on my own. Even the people in the office are sick of their manager bringing them gifts of fish!"

Well! Sherlock Holmes alert! He'd told me all I needed to know about himself.

He didn't have a cat of his own to help with the fish, he had a good job in an office and most importantly, he wasn't married.

He would do very nicely for Cathy, in my opinion. But how was I going to introduce them? Forcing him to trip over me as he passed her gate would be a bit unsubtle, I felt.

I said my farewells and went home to think about it.

They say the best ideas are the simplest, and mine was a stroke of genius. Although I would have to sacrifice the reputation of being a good citizen in order to carry out my plan, it couldn't fail to work.

The next weekend when he came walking past our house with his knapsack of fish, I jumped down from the gatepost and followed him closely.

"Hello, kitty," he said cheerfully. "So this is where you live? And are you coming home with me for a fish supper again?"

Indeed I was! I lulled him into a sense of false security by sitting on the kitchen counter and purring loudly while I watched him clean his fish. There was one particularly big silvery one he was very proud of.

"Where're my scales?" he muttered, looking in the cupboard. "This beauty's at least three pounds."

Quick as a flash I snatched it up and left via the kitchen window. With great difficulty, I might add, because it was much heavier than I expected. I staggered along the pavement and rushed indoors to Cathy, dragging my prize behind me through the cat-flap.

"Hey! You thief! Bring that back!"

I could hear my fisherman friend shouting furiously three doors away. The next thing, there was a loud banging on the front door. Aha, exactly as I had anticipated.

Cathy opened the door, puzzled.

"Your cat's just stolen my fish!" he said.

Then he sort of stopped and looked at her and smiled. "Sorry, I didn't mean to startle you. It's not that important, actually. I'm Mike Harrison, by the way, your next door neighbour, almost."

Honestly, if he were a cat he'd have been purring.

"Cathy Burnett. But I'm sure Baker would never steal food."

That was sweet of her, defending me.

But she changed her mind when they discovered the remains of his delicious three pound carp tucked behind the television. Well, I couldn't let it just sit there, could I?

"I can't believe Baker did something like this, I'm terribly sorry."

She apologized very prettily and Mike kept saying things like "It doesn't matter at all" and "I've plenty more fish where that one came from," and I could see he just wanted to stay and chat to Cathy.

She shooed me out and I heard her offering him a cup of coffee, so I walked around the house and came back in through the kitchen window to listen in.

"So you're a fisherman?" she asked. "My dad used to go fishing every weekend and I loved going with him."

"Really? Most girls get bored just sitting around on the river bank."

"Oh, I liked to fish as well."

Even from the next room I could sense the happy vibrations between them.

"You did? Perhaps—I mean—maybe you'd like to come with me one Sunday?"

I'd known he'd be perfect for Cathy. Mike was completely different from that awful Rob—not pushy and overconfident.

"I think I'd like that very much."

Aha, I thought, listening with satisfaction. It's all worked out according to plan.

I could see years of fish suppers for Mike and me stretching ahead.

BURNING BRIDGES

Sarah Doebereiner

ON THE RIDE HOME I felt numb. There was this deep, vast sadness buried underneath the surface. I kept shoveling anger on top of it so I wouldn't have to feel the grief. It's a short trip from the veterinary hospital back to my house. Despite everything that happened, when I opened the door, I expected her to be there. I listened for the tap – tap –tap of her claws against the tile in the kitchen. I watched for the gentle flurry of fur that shook around her like a sash when she got excited. Silence.

I tried to throw my keys on the kitchen table, but they fell short. I didn't even pick them up. My coat and purse slid off of my shoulder and to the floor. There were phone calls to make, statuses to update. I had to find a way to tell people about what had happened— only I couldn't say it out loud. Once it was out there, I couldn't ever take it back. Then it would be real. Ginny was dead—not just dead, but murdered.

Laughter floated through a slit at the bottom of the kitchen window. Layers of paint on top of paint prevented it from closing completely. I cringed at the

47

noise. The loud, angry drunk attached to that voice killed my dog. There was no doubt in my mind. He always shouted at her. He complained about living next to a single woman with a dog. He got arrested last year for knocking over the mailbox of the people three houses down after their kids left their bicycles in front of his driveway one afternoon. I pictured him there laughing at his television while my baby lay dead on an ice cold table.

I guess—I guess I sort of lost it. I grabbed a leftover baked potato from the counter—a remnant of yesterday's unfinished lunch. It still had the skin on it, but I could feel it squish gently in my hand. Thinking about it now, I'm not sure why it made such perfect sense at the time. I grabbed a shoebox full of what I called my survival kit, where I kept things like hammers, screwdrivers, screws, and nails. I picked the largest nails I could find. Four inches maybe? I don't know. I have small hands, but they stretched up towards my middle finger when I held them in my palm.

I pushed them into the potato. They went all the way through and stuck out the other side. The coarse, grainy pulp held the nails in place without difficulty. The density was perfectly suited to it. I put so many in that the potato looked more like a hedgehog when I was done. It was overkill, and I see that now. It's just... that laugh. Every time I heard it I wanted to hurt him. I wanted to do something to make him experience the pain he caused me.

Of course I never intended him to eat it. He was a bastard, but even as upset as I was, I'd never have killed him. Even drunk, hell even blind, you would never mistake it for edible. I put the potato into a plain paper bag. The sun had begun to set. People were already home from school and work. They would probably be settling down to dinner. The streets were empty. I put the bag on his porch, lit it on fire, and rang the bell before dashing back to my own house. It's an old trick, the poop bag, but I gave it my own twist.

I watched through the front window. I saw the door open, he was unsteady on his feet. He brought his bare foot down on the bag, and screamed in shock. The sound quickly turned to something more frantic as the pain hit. He toppled over and shouted. He always shouted.

The nails in the potato stuck in his foot, but they did something else too. They pinned the flaming bag to the bottom of his pants. Before I knew it, his clothes caught fire. It spread so much faster than I would have thought. Light from the flames danced along his body so delicately that it might have been beautiful if it wasn't so horrific.

I stood there gaping out the window with a dumbfounded look on my face for longer than I should have. No one came. No one helped. He was the most hated man on the block, so everyone just ignored him. I grabbed a towel off of its place hanging from the handle of the refrigerator. I twisted the knob on the sink and let some water run onto it before I raced outside. I patted, beat, and smacked the damp cloth on him until the fire went out. The smell of charred skin crept up my nostrils. I screamed, and when I screamed people came.

Soon, flashing lights emerged on our street. Curious eyes peered out of their doors. Hands clasped me on the shoulders. A policeman with kind eyes took my statement and patted me on the back. He smiled. I was a hero. They had dozens of complaints for this address. If I hadn't stepped in when I did, then the man would surely have died. I saved his life. They even did a story about it in the paper warning people to watch out for kids spreading flaming bags of nail potatoes as a prank. I never told them what really happened. I never told anyone. As far as my friends and family knew, Ginny died of old age. The vet told me not to feel guilty, that dogs were adept at getting into things they shouldn't. Her belly was full of chocolate, but it wasn't my fault. The vet stressed that. Only, it really wasn't my fault. I just couldn't say it.

The old drunk never came home. He survived though. He more or less recovered and went to live with his daughter. She sold the house. Rumor in the neighborhood was that she had been trying to do it for years. I was so happy that he was gone. I knew I should feel bad for what I did, but I didn't. If I felt any remorse at all, it was feeling bad for not feeling bad. It's been over a year now.

***

"And now you are looking for forgiveness?" the shrink asks.

"Not exactly," I respond.

"Are you thinking about turning yourself in?"

I take a deep breath and let it out as a sigh. "Actually, I've been thinking about getting a new dog. Losing Ginny was horrible, and nothing can ever replace her. I went through a lot, but I think I might be ready. Is it too soon to think about getting another dog?"

A long pause floats between us. I wonder for a moment if I made a mistake coming here.

"My cousin's Pug/Chihuahua mix just had puppies, and he is looking for homes for them. He calls them Chugs," the shrink says. He chuckles lightly. I smile and ask if he has any pictures.

KATELYNN THE MYTHIC MOUSER

Mary E. Lowd

JENNA WAS ALMOST ASLEEP when she felt the weight of a cat plop onto the end of her bed. She turned on the lamp on the bedside table and saw Katelynn, her aunt's dirt-brown tabby, sitting on the bed's patchwork comforter.

A tiny mouse hung by its tail from Katelynn's mouth, twisting and squirming, desperate to get away.

"Oh! Katelynn, thank you!"

Jenna crawled out of bed and hurried to set up her candles on the dresser beside the terrarium. She sprinkled salt in a circle around the candles and crumbled dried lavender into the flames. Then she opened her aunt's spell book to a page with an ornate drawing of Pegasus and an illusion spell handwritten in cramped, cursive letters.

"Okay Katelynn, I'm ready. Don't let it get away."

The tabby jumped off the bed, trotted across the room, and then leapt delicately onto the dresser. Jenna lifted the mesh lid of the terrarium, and Katelynn dropped the terrified mouse inside.

Jenna and Katelynn watched the mouse cower, too afraid to explore its new home. The other inhabitants of the terrarium, however, came out from their cardboard and colorful-plastic hiding places, drawn by curiosity—first, a perfect little unicorn as white as lily petals; then a serpentine, winged dragon as black as the night sky; and, finally, a golden-furred gryphon with a tufted tail and clacky beak. Each creature was the size of a mouse.

Jenna chanted the words from the spell book, just as her aunt had taught her. The light from the candles grew taller, stretching up from the wicks and curling through the air like glowing smoke. The threads of light tangled in the air, sewing themselves up into the glowing image of Pegasus. Jenna finished chanting and blew the candles out, severing the illusion from them.

For a moment, the illusory Pegasus hung in the air. Then it condensed into a point of light and danced like a will-o-the-wisp into the terrarium. Finally, it landed on the cowering mouse's forehead, transforming the mouse into a downy, white Pegasus, a perfect match for the unicorn.

Jenna grabbed Katelynn and hugged her around her furry middle. "I didn't think you'd catch the last mouse in time!"

Purrs overflowed the tabby, as if Jenna had squeezed them out of her.

Jenna put Katelynn back on the dresser and then swept the salt and lavender into a trash bin. She reached to close the spell book, but Katelynn batted at her hand playfully.

"I'll play with you tomorrow Katelynn, before my parents come to take me home."

Jenna had spent the summer at her aunt's house,

learning magic. Her parents didn't know about the magic. They just wanted her out of the way while they finished up their big, boring work project.

Jenna pulled her hand away from the book, and Katelynn pounced on the yellowed pages. She nosed and pawed, flipping through the pages, until the book lay open to the illusion for Hydra.

Katelynn sat proudly by the emerald green illustration of a serpent with many, many hissing heads. Aunt Molly said that Katelynn sometimes played with snakes in the yard. Unlike mice, she was never able to catch them. She'd opened the spell book to this page before.

"All right," Jenna said. "If you catch me one more mouse, I'll make Hydra. But you'd better do it tonight. I'm leaving in the morning."

***

Jenna woke up to Katelynn pawing her face. It was still dark, but, as her eyes adjusted, Jenna made out the shape of another squirming mouse hanging only inches from her face.

"Ugh! Katelynn! Get that away from me."

Having been properly acknowledged, the tabby jumped off the bed, crossed the room, and leapt onto the dresser again. She pawed at the lid of the terrarium, catching the mesh in her claws.

Jenna laughed. "Silly cat." But she got out of bed and did all the work of casting an illusion spell again.

***

In the morning, Jenna woke to find Katelynn still

on the dresser, staring intently at the tiny, mythical creatures inside her terrarium. She'd never heard Katelynn purr so loudly.

The purring ended when Katelynn saw Jenna bring out her suitcase. As Jenna packed her clothes, Katelynn repeatedly hid in the suitcase and had to be dragged back out. When the suitcase was finally zipped shut, Katelynn yowled miserably.

"I told you that I have to go," Jenna said.

Katelynn skulked away and hid behind the terrarium.

Aunt Molly came to the door. "Are you all packed?" she asked.

Jenna looked around. With all her things packed back in her suitcase, the room looked like an ordinary guest room again, except for the terrarium filled with tiny, mythical creatures. "I guess so," she said. "I don't think Katelynn wants me to leave."

"I'm not surprised. She doesn't get much attention when you're not here."

Jenna couldn't help thinking about how sad Katelynn would be when she realized that the terrarium was leaving too. Aunt Molly had asked, and her parents had said it was okay for her to bring home a terrarium filled with mice. They wouldn't be able to see the illusion spells that turned them into a unicorn, dragon, gryphon, Hydra, and Pegasus.

"I wish I could bring Katelynn with me..." Jenna felt bad as soon as she said it. Katelynn was her aunt's cat, not hers.

"Your mom said yes to mice— they stay in their terrarium. She wouldn't be okay with a cat."

The way Aunt Molly said it, she almost sounded like she would be okay with Jenna taking Katelynn.

"Wouldn't you miss her?"

Aunt Molly shrugged. "She doesn't like me much. She sleeps all day on the back of the couch and growls if I disturb her."

Katelynn was nothing like that for Jenna. She played with string, snuggled on the bed with her at night, and followed her all around the house. The idea of leaving Katelynn behind to be a grouchy, lonely cat was heartbreaking.

"What if..." Jenna thought about all the spells she'd learned that summer. They were mostly illusions, a few that could heat or cool water, and one that made her hair braid itself. But Aunt Molly knew many more. "Do you have a spell that could shrink Katelynn down to fit in my terrarium?"

Aunt Molly's brow furrowed in thought. "Maybe. Let me check."

Jenna followed Aunt Molly into her library. All the walls were covered in book shelves, each shelf filled end to end with books. Even more books were stacked sideways on top of the others. There were two chairs, each with an end table beside it piled high in books, too. Jenna had spent a lot of time in the library, but she hadn't been able to figure out any organization scheme to the books. Romance novels stood next to calculus text books. This year's bestsellers stood next to dusty old, handwritten spell books.

Aunt Molly walked around the room, occasionally putting her hand to a shelf, and finally pulled out one of the spell books. She flipped through the pages, settled on one, and said, "This would work. But I don't have time before your parents get here."

"Can I look?" Jenna nearly tripped over Katelynn who was weaving between her legs and purring. She picked the tabby up and crossed the room to look at Aunt Molly's open spell book.

The list of ingredients wasn't too hard— fresh mint, a vial of peridot gems, thorns from the stem of an unopened rose, cinnamon incense, and almond oil. The chant looked difficult, much more difficult than any of the chants Jenna had done so far.

"Why don't you have time? We could do this right now," Jenna said.

"I can't just cast this on Katelynn. It doesn't only make an animal smaller—there has to be balance, so it makes another animal bigger."

"Maybe Katelynn could catch another mouse." Jenna smiled down at the tabby purring in her arms; golden cat eyes smiled up at her. "She's a terrific mouser."

"I don't want a giant mouse running around my house, thank you very much."

"A cat-sized mouse?" Jenna asked.

"No, probably just a rat-sized mouse, but I still don't want one." Aunt Molly shut the spell book and put it on one of the piles of books. "Tell you what, I'll figure something out, and I'll bring Katelynn to you in a few weeks."

Jenna didn't want to wait a few weeks. Katelynn wouldn't understand it was only a few weeks and would think Jenna had abandoned her. But Aunt Molly gave her the look that said *this conversation is over*, and left the room.

Katelynn jumped out of Jenna's arms and batted the spell book off of the pile. It fell open on the floor, and Katelynn nosed it back to the page with the shrinking spell.

"Okay," Jenna said. "I won't give up, but if Aunt

Molly says 'no mice,' then no mice. You'll have to catch something else."

Jenna went to the kitchen and got a vial of peridot gems, a small bottle of almond oil, and cinnamon incense from one of the spell supply drawers. She slipped the glass vial, bottle, and incense sticks in her pocket. Then, she went outside to the garden, Katelynn following her.

When Jenna had first seen Aunt Molly's garden, it looked like a wild mess of greenery, an untamed jungle. But, over the summer, she'd learned to see the hidden structure—every plant was useful, and every inch of space was filled with plants.

Jenna waded her way between the waist-high lavender and rosemary shrubs to the brilliant green mint plants. She ripped off several sprigs, and their bright smell sharpened the air, overpowering all the other scents mingling together. Aunt Molly's garden always smelled amazing.

Aunt Molly had a rose bush of every color, each of them lost in a tangle of shrubs and herbs. They weren't for being beautiful; their blooms and thorns were for working spells.

Jenna made her way to the orange roses first, but all of the flowers were in wide bloom. She heard a rustling in the shrubs and looked down to see Katelynn with a mouse wriggling in her mouth.

"No mice," Jenna said.

Katelynn flattened her ears, dropped the mouse, and disappeared back into the greenery with her tail swishing angrily.

Jenna heard a car driving up the gravel road out front. That would be her parents. She needed to hurry.

The yellow and red roses were in full bloom too,

but, on the white rose bush, she found a perfect, sweet little bud. Pressing her thumb against each thorn on its stem, she snapped them all off. She cradled the needle-sharp thorns carefully in the palm of her hand.

"Meow!" Katelynn snagged her claws in the fabric of Jenna's pants. Then, she stared intently with her golden eyes at the rose bush.

Jenna followed her gaze: a tiny flutter of red-and-black wings landed on the edge of a rose leaf. A ladybug was small enough that Aunt Molly couldn't object to making it larger. Jenna gently picked up the ladybug and placed it in her thorn-filled palm. She closed her hand loosely around the precious collection.

Back inside, Jenna fended off hugs from her parents and hurried into the guest room. Katelynn followed her like a shadow.

She locked the door, propped Aunt Molly's spell book against the terrarium, and began following its directions very precisely. She poured the green peridot gems out in a circle. She put the cinnamon incense in a censer and lit it. She arranged the rose thorns at the corners and intersections of an imaginary star inside the circle of peridot. She crushed the mint leaves, wadding it into a ball and placed it at the center of the imaginary star.

Next she put a single drop of almond oil on the ladybug in her palm. Katelynn's nose wrinkled, but she let Jenna put a drop of almond oil in the fur between her ears.

Then Jenna took a deep breath and began chanting.

Nothing happened. Jenna worried that she'd got the pronunciation wrong, but she kept going, saying the words as clearly as she could.

Finally, she realized that the smell of mint and

cinnamon was growing stronger, much stronger than anything she'd smelled before. The scent was so strong, it was as if she could see the green and red-brown color of the smells in the air.

The smell was sharp like peppermint. Then, suddenly, it was cool like spearmint.

Katelynn meowed. Her voice was much higher. Jenna felt giddy looking at the tiny mouse-sized cat on her dresser. The ladybug in her hand was the size of a quarter. She couldn't believe she'd pulled off such a difficult spell.

Katelynn jumped from the dresser onto Jenna's shoulder, purred, and bumped her head against Jenna's.

Knocking on the door. "Hey, Jenna, it's time to go," her mother said.

"Just a minute!" Jenna called. "I have to do one last thing."

Jenna cleaned up the supplies from the shrinking spell and set up the supplies for one last illusion spell. She ignored her parents knocking and complaints while she cast a reverse illusion on Katelynn—it didn't change how Jenna saw her, but her parents would see only another mouse.

Jenna let her impatient parents into the room. She held the ladybug out to her aunt. "See this beetle I found?"

"That looks a lot like a ladybug," Aunt Molly said.

Jenna beamed with pride, and her aunt shook her head knowingly.

"Couldn't wait two weeks, huh? Mind if I keep the ladybug? I mean, beetle. That might actually be my kind of pet."

"What are you talking about?" Jenna's father asked.

"Nothing," Jenna said, placing the giant ladybug in her aunt's palm. Then, turning to her mother, she said, "Look at my mice!"

Jenna showed her parents the terrarium. Pegasus and the unicorn were racing each other around the edges. The gryphon was preening her golden feathers. And the dragon flared her ebony wings, mock-fighting with the hissing emerald heads of the Hydra.

Jenna's parents oohed appreciatively, almost as if they could really see.

"Okay, kiddo, let's get this circus out to the car," her mother said.

Her father said, "I'll carry your suitcase."

Before picking up the terrarium to take it to the car, Jenna placed her final mythical creature inside. She thought that Katelynn, a simple brown tabby cat, looked perfectly at home with the others. The smile in Katelynn's golden eyes agreed.

THE LITTLEST WEREWOLF

Ed Burkley

THE MOON WILL BE FULL tonight. I can smell its pull on the tide. The air gets saltier when the moon has its way with the sea. I can feel its pull on me too. And tonight maybe, just maybe, I will finally change.

What's the rush you might ask? It's the coming war that prompts my haste. I want to be ready for when *they* come. But wait, always one to rush a story, I get ahead of myself. I'll get to that problem soon enough. First, you might wonder why I haven't changed already. Well, I'm still young. It's not surprising to still be in my present form at my age. I just have to be patient and one night, under a full moon, I'll transform. And oh, to have two large arms able to lift impossible things, to slice through my foes. That day can't come soon enough. Once I saw my parents shred our dinner, slicing though meat, hands ending in silvery sharp blades. The flesh fell to the floor and I ate the sweet taste of our fallen victim. It was so wonderful, a bliss that my regular food never brings. I want to be big and strong like my parents so I too can stand triumphant over my prey. I've even seen my dad tear apart some of our meals with his bare hands. Such power!

You see I'm not that strong or big compared to others of my kind, even others of my same age. When I go to the park to play with them, I get picked on a lot. Tabitha just sticks her nose up at me. And Frank, well he's just a bulldog. Every time I arrive at the park he runs up and tackles me to the ground. Frank thinks it funny. I don't. I try and tell my parents that I don't like it when the others treat me this way but they don't ever seem to hear me. I think it's their way of making me tough. I do my best to keep up with the pack, but like I said, I'm small. The others tease me and call me the runt of the litter. Some even steal my things. Like the other day, Thomas came right up and took my ball and ran off with it. They think it's funny, but I don't find the humor in it. But one day soon, under the glare of a full moon, I will turn and become big like my dad. Then we'll see who's a runt.

You are probably wondering how I found out I was a werewolf. Well, it happened one evening while I sat on the couch with my mother, snuggled in my favorite blanket. My mother showed me images that moved of those who looked like me and under a full moon they changed. I was terrified at first, but soon saw the blessing in their strength. I too wanted to change. And I knew one day I would. I would change and one day look as my parents do, big and strong and menacing; to be such a being. But I would soon discover our kind was not alone.

It was when I was out walking with Max awhile back. Max is my friend, probably my only true friend. He hasn't transformed yet either and doesn't make fun of me. He asked if I had seen them yet. I said that I didn't know what he was talking about.

The *creatures*, he said panting, his eyes wide. I thought it a bit dramatic and gave him a noncommittal laugh.

No really, he said. There was a war coming and we were under attack.

Well, I said, I haven't seen any of these beasts.

He looked me dead in the eyes and said, you will my friend, you will. When you least expect it, they come from the trees. I've seen them with my own eyes, he said, then added, do you ever look up into the trees?

I said no.

Then you need to, he said, that's when you'll see them. They are waiting up there, gathering their forces and someday soon they will pounce! And with that he jumped on me. We laughed. I thought he was just joking. That was until I finally saw them with my own two eyes.

Soon after my conversation with Max, my parents started the training. They never told me what it was about, just had me practice attacking a stuffed prop that was supposed to look like these creatures—long and furry, little claws, black eyes, and a twitching tail that thrashed about. Even with all the training though, I didn't really believe the creatures existed. Then, one day, they came. I will never forget it, partly because I saw more than one kind of beast that day.

It was just like Max said. They came… from the trees. It was the clicking noise above that first drew my attention. Then I saw them, yes *them*. There was more than one. They ran down the tree almost defying gravity, swirling around its trunk as they descended. Such foul creatures with little beastly claws, mangy fur and the eyes a soulless black. They descended the tree and then approached my house. I looked for my parents but they must have still been inside. Of course the beasts would pick such a time to attack.

They saw me. We locked eyes and before they could act I seized my moment and lunged at the one closest to me. He was quick, demonically fast. But my advancement scared him and his friend off. So I was satisfied in what I considered a victory.

Then a screech came from up in the tree, this time not from one of the beady-eyed vermin but from something even stranger. It was black with yellow eyes that stared into my very being. I leapt at it and, seeing that I had made its position, the monster with a maddening cry spread its large wings and took flight. Only then, when accompanied by its brethren in the air, did I see just how outnumbered I truly was. Never again would I make that mistake.

And now I know a war is coming, between our kind and those in the trees. Now I don't *want* to change, I *need* to change. I must be ready when the battle descends. My pack has stepped up the patrolling of our neighborhood. I have trained so hard and am ready. My only concern is that I won't have turned by the time they do attack. Even now, as I stroll through the streets with my parents, I must keep a watchful eye. As the sun goes down, casting strange shadows from the trees, I worry. The warm breeze fills my lungs. But my eyes are always on the trees. Does the wind move their branches or is there something more that moves within them, something vile, something horrid? I hope I'm ready. I hope I'll change in time.

As we walk, someone approaches my parents and me. I don't recognize them, but my parents don't seem alarmed so I too relax. Then they ask my mom something.

***

"Oh how cute," the blonde lady says to Melissa and Ed as she reaches down to pet their dog. "What's his name?"

"Fizzgig," Melissa replies.

"That's an interesting name." The lady raises an eyebrow.

"Yeah, his name comes from one of our favorite childhood movies," Melissa says. "An old Jim Henson film. Both my husband and I loved it so much as children we wanted to name our first dog after one of its dog-like creatures."

The woman nods. As she finishes her petting, she stands up and asks, "Is he a puppy?"

"No," Ed replies, "that's as big as he'll get." Then with a smile adds, "But don't tell him that."

"Wow, so little—"

"But tough," Ed is quick to add. "Like a little tank."

"And what breed is he?"

"He's a Norwich terrier," Melissa answers as she smiles at Fizzgig.

"Well he's simply adorable. Too cute," the lady says, looking down at the dog. "I mean just look at his eyes, he has such soulful eyes, the way he looks directly into yours. It's almost like a person is behind them. They almost seem like human eyes."

"That's what we always tell each other," Melissa says. "It's like there's a person trapped in there just waiting to get out."

Melissa and Ed smile at the woman, then wave goodbye and continue to walk down the street of their quaint neighborhood, the sidewalks lined with pecan and oak trees.

***

I listen to my parents and the other talk, but of course I don't understand them. I haven't gone through the transformation yet. I don't speak their tongue. But soon I will. For tonight is another full moon and I can feel its pull, its pull on the trees, on me and maybe, just maybe, I will finally change.

HELLHOUND

Amanda Bergloff

"NO ONE WANTS A HELLHOUND," my friend
Zach said.

"Says you," I replied. "I want one."

"You're crazy," he laughed.

It was the year of my seventh birthday, and that's
all I wanted. I had seen a picture of one in a book I got
from the library called *The Big Book of Unnatural
Animals and Other Oddities That Kids Wonder About.*
I renewed the book four times before I was told that I
couldn't any longer because other people might want to
check it out, too.

"Besides," Zach continued, "there's no such thing
as a hellhound."

"Yes, there is." I corrected him. "I saw it in a
book."

"That was fake," he said.

"Well, that's what I'm getting for my birthday next
week," I said. "My Uncle Bob always brings me things
I ask for."

"Hmmph. I'll bet you five bucks that he *doesn't*
bring it and that you *don't* get a hellhound for your

68

birthday."

I didn't hesitate for a minute. "You're on." I spit in my palm and held it out for him to seal our bet. Zach didn't want to shake my spit-filled hand. He punched me in the arm instead.

"Okay, big shot. I'll see you next week." He rode off on his bike.

Zach was ten and the neighborhood know-it-all. Although he was my friend, I couldn't wait to prove him wrong. Hellhounds were real, and I was going to get one.

I had memorized everything about them from that picture book. I read and re-read the section called "Ghost Dogs and Fearsome Hellhounds," which detailed the lives of the creatures. I learned that although a ghost dog was the spirit of a dog who had died and came back to haunt its former owners, a hellhound was a dog who could paralyze people with fear if they looked into its red eyes or heard its growl in the night. Hellhounds were almost impossible to train and did not play nicely with others. Unlike ghost dogs who just wanted to float around and play ghost-fetch, hellhounds wanted to tear things up, and chase souls of the people who the owner of the hellhound didn't like. Hellhounds were always black, while ghost dogs were always white. Hellhounds had a bad attitude, while ghost dogs had no attitude.

Clearly, hellhounds were the way to go for me as a pet.

When my mom told me Uncle Bob was on the phone to talk to me about my birthday, I jumped at the chance to tell him what I wanted.

"Hellhound, huh?" he asked. "I heard they're really hard to house train and always bite through a leash if you take them on a walk."

"I don't care," I replied. "It would listen to me because I wouldn't make it do anything it didn't want to do."

Uncle Bob chuckled. "Sounds like you've done your research. I'll see what I can do. No promises though, okay?"

Uncle Bob always said that he would see what he could do, and then he always came through for me. Mom couldn't understand why I'd even want such a thing.

"You know they're not real, right?" she asked.

I just smiled and said, "I guess so." I knew that was what she wanted to hear, but that's not what I really thought.

A few days before my birthday, Zach rode up on his bike and blocked my path on the sidewalk. "Did your uncle get you the hellhound yet?"

"No, because my birthday is this Saturday. I have to wait until then."

Zach rolled his eyes. "Whatever. Remember, our bet is still on. I'll collect my five dollars on Sunday." He punched me in the arm and took off on his bike down the street.

Zach was definitely the type of person that would be paralyzed if he ever looked into the red eyes of a hellhound. At the very least, I thought I would have my new hellhound growl outside his bedroom window one night, so he would be paralyzed in bed and have bad dreams. I then thought about how I would spend the five dollars I collected from him on a new red leash for my fearsome pet.

The night before my birthday, I couldn't sleep. Thoughts of my uncle walking into my house with a big black hellhound wearing a red bow around its neck kept playing through my mind. My mother's mouth would drop open at the realization that a hellhound was indeed real, and she would apologize for ever doubting me. My hellhound would run up to me and lick my face with its long black tongue, and since it was mine, I would not be paralyzed when I looked into its red eyes because a hellhound would love its owner and never scare them. As I lay there waiting to fall asleep, I laughed when I thought of Zach handing me five bucks when he lost our bet. I would punch him in the arm when I took it from him.

The morning of my birthday, my mom made me my favorite breakfast of brown sugar on toast with bacon on the side. My family was going to gather in the afternoon for a birthday celebration. I knew my mom and grandparents would get me some toys, books, and games, but my Uncle Bob was the one who would be bringing the gift I was most excited about.

Everyone arrived for my birthday lunch, except for Uncle Bob. I could barely eat the pizza in front of me because I was worried that he wouldn't show up. He still wasn't there when it was time to open my presents. I was afraid to ask my mom if he was coming at all. I didn't want to hear her say that he wasn't.

He finally walked in the door as I ripped the bright birthday paper off a present from my grandma. It was a book about dinosaurs and a spaceship. I thanked her, and my heart sank as Uncle Bob sat down next to my mom. There was no big black dog by his side with a red bow around its neck. Not even a book-sized wrapped gift.

I opened the rest of my presents and forced a smile on my face when I thanked everyone. My mom said it was time to light the candles on my birthday cake, but my Uncle Bob stopped her.

"Wait a minute," he said, "I haven't given my gift, yet." He pushed the torn wrapping paper and presents that surrounded me out of the way so he could sit down in front of me.

"Before I give you your present," he said solemnly, "I have to ask you a few questions."

I could feel my heart beat faster and I nodded.

"What you asked for isn't so easy to get. It took me quite a while."

My mouth got dry.

"This kind of gift comes with a lot of responsibilities. It's not something you can just get tired of and not take care of anymore, because you'll have it for a long time."

My hands started to shake.

"Are you willing to accept the consequences that come along with having this type of present? They're quite serious, you know. I hope that book of yours talked about it."

My whole body was shaking at this point, and I could barely hold back my shout of "Yes!"

Uncle Bob smiled and winked. "Then close your eyes until I tell you to open them."

I closed my eyes and froze in place. I heard Uncle Bob get up and open the front door. I could tell he went outside, then walked back in and shut the door. The air in the room felt different to me. There was something else with him. Something that would help me collect five dollars from Zach when I showed it to him tomorrow.

"You can open your eyes now," Uncle Bob said.

I took a deep breath and opened them. I saw the

big red bow first.

"Oh, it's so cute!" Mom exclaimed.

The fluffy gray puppy with one white ear jumped into my lap and wagged its puppy tail.

It was not the big black dog I was expecting. Its puppy eyes were not red, and its puppy tongue was not black.

Mom said "Let me get a picture of you and Uncle Bob with your new dog." I sat there with the non-hellhound in my lap while Uncle Bob smiled next to me and gave a thumbs up for the photo.

My birthday cake was brought out while the puppy ran around the room. I blew out the candles and didn't bother to make a wish when my mom said to. I poked at the piece of cake in front of me with my fork while everyone laughed when the puppy jumped into my lap and tried to lick my plate with its very pink, non-black tongue.

I stared at Uncle Bob. My lower lip began to tremble, and before I could stop myself, I burst into tears.

"But Uncle Bob, this isn't the hellhound I asked for! It's just an ordinary puppy!" I wailed.

My mom told me to stop crying and that I should be grateful.

"It's okay," he said to her. "I thought there was a chance he would be disappointed at first."

The non-hellhound in my lap began to lick the tears off my face which tickled. I was able to catch my breath then and stop crying.

Uncle Bob faced me. "I thought your book would have mentioned that hellhounds are different when they're puppies."

I shook my head no.

"Oh, then that explains it. You see," he continued, "hellhounds are not like ordinary dogs even though they may look like one. They grow at their own pace and have to make sure that they fit with their owner, and that their bond will be unbreakable. Do you understand?"

I sniffed and nodded my head yes.

The fluffy gray puppy in front of me with the one white ear snuggled close to my heart. It really was cute, even if it wasn't big and black.

Before he left, Uncle Bob helped me fix a box up for my new puppy to sleep in, even though the puppy slept on my bed that night and every night after.

I hugged my uncle and thanked him when he left. He meant well even if it wasn't the present I had asked for.

Zach laughed his head off the next day when I handed him five dollars. He got a good look at the puppy at the end of its leash and said, "Told ya." When he tried to punch me in the arm, my puppy barked and nipped at his leg. He shrugged and rode off on his bike.

Birthdays came and went after that. Memories blurred and ran together. My fluffy puppy grew into my devoted grown up dog. I even gave it a friendly name that people smiled at when I told them.

I realized as the years went by that the dreams of a seven year old evolve into the realities of adulthood. They bear little resemblance to one another, yet there is still a faint glimmer of what they used to be. Life and relationships can change, however the bond that I shared with my dog stayed the same and was unbreakable.

And on one of my adult birthdays, I woke to find red eyes staring at me in the dark. They did not paralyze me with fear because I knew that a true hellhound only has love for its owner. The large, now black dog with one white ear, had grown at its own pace and was now ready for its true calling. Its low-throated growl also didn't paralyze me because it had a familiarity to it. It contained the same sound of trust it used to have when the creature before me was still in its gray form. It came forward and licked my face, just as it had always done, only now its tongue was black, not pink anymore.

I understood and heard its true name spoken in my mind, not the temporary one I had given it, and I spoke it out loud, so it would know I was ready.

It turns out Zach was partially correct all those years ago when he said that the facts about hellhounds in *The Big Book of Unnatural Animals and Other Oddities That Kids Wonder About,* were fake. The book had said that fearsome hellhounds wanted to tear things up and chase the souls of people who the owner of the hellhound didn't like. Turns out hellhounds reap the souls of *all* people, not just the ones their owners don't like.

You see, there are consequences to owning a hellhound, as my Uncle Bob had said. It comes with a lot of responsibilities and is not something you can just get tired of because you'll have it for a long time. I was willing to accept the seriousness of owning one back then, and I still am now, and I will be a Reaper with a hellhound bound by my side, helping it take souls for as long as time allows.

THE LOCKET

R. J. Meldrum

MIDNIGHT. ALL WAS quiet as Caroline headed back to her apartment, the streetlights guiding her as she walked along the wet pavement. Luckily it had stopped raining before she left the bar where she worked. Something in the gutter attracted her attention. It was full of dirty water and detritus, leaves, plastic wrapping, and cigarette butts, but there was something else too; a silver object. She knelt, rolled up her sleeve and grabbed it, but the object slid from her grasp.

Carefully she tried again, she had come this far, she might as well carry on. Her fingers made better contact, enough to be able to lift it out. She looked down at her find, a silver locket. She clicked it open, revealing an empty interior. Caroline shivered, suddenly cold. She put it into her pocket and headed home, unaware a dark shape now followed her.

Back at her apartment, empty and dark because her flatmate was out, Caroline slipped into bed without turning on any lights. She put the locket on her bedside cabinet, feeling its smoothness. She felt the urge to keep it close; much the same way she had felt the urge to rescue it from the gutter. She turned her head into the pillow and slept.

Something woke her. The clock said it was two a.m. She sat up, mentally checking she had locked the front door. Memory confirmed she had. There was a scratching at her bedroom door, the sort of sound a small dog or cat would make. The problem was neither Caroline nor her flatmate Andrea owned such a creature.

Puzzled more than scared, she got up and went to the door. The scratching continued. Caroline paused briefly, unsure whether or not to open the door. What could it be, this mysterious visitor? She saw her hand, unconsciously, depress the metal handle and the door opened slightly. Something entered her bedroom, but in the darkness Caroline had a hard time making out what it was. It was clearly an animal of some kind, but what? It jumped onto her bed. Caroline clicked on the main room light, uncertain she was entirely comfortable with some unknown creature making itself at home on her duvet. When her eyes had adjusted, she saw there was nothing there. Well, not quite nothing. Her duvet was moving, little depressions appearing and disappearing. Indentations that formed a circle. Caroline had been brought up in a household full of animals so she could place the movement; it was the circling motion dogs performed before settling to sleep. Something invisible was making a bed for itself on her duvet. Caroline reached out towards the unseen animal and her hand touched soft fur. She sat on the edge of her bed. A cold muzzle nudged into her hand. Instinctively Caroline began stroking the creature's head and flank. It moved into the curve of her leg and settled; she could feel its warmth and a tiny heart beating against her skin.

"A ghost," she muttered to herself.

She wasn't troubled by the discovery. Unlike most people, Caroline was quite comfortable with the notion of the spirit world; her whole life had been spent in the presence of the supernatural. Her mum was a professional medium and Caroline's childhood had been filled with readings, trances, and séances. Her dead uncle shared the family house and a large part of her childhood had involved her mother telling her to roll down her sleeves or tidy up the dishes because her Uncle Fred didn't approve. She had inherited some of her mother's perception and, sensing that this spirit was no threat, she went back to bed. Sleep quickly overcame her.

The next morning Caroline woke to find something was standing on her upper chest. Her hand sought and found a furry head that immediately started to lick her fingers. A dog, she decided. Definitely.

"So, what shall I call you, my new friend?"

No response. Did ghost dogs bark, she wondered.

"I don't think Rover will quite do, will it?"

She considered various names, then decided.

"Well, you are a ghost, so let's call you Boo."

A tongue licked her hand and there was an endearingly cute snuffling noise.

"Ah, you approve. Good."

One question arose in her mind.

"Are you a girl or a boy?"

Her hands sought the answer.

"A girl. Good."

Over breakfast Caroline mulled over the situation. A ghost dog was a most welcome pet; it didn't break the lease, nor did it entail long walks in the rain or scooping various unmentionables. In many ways, Caroline wished she'd sought such a companion before. She found herself glancing down, even though there was nothing to see.

"Where did you come from?"

Her mind drifted to the bedside table and the locket.

"Ah," she said. "I opened it, didn't I?"

There was a snuffle from under the kitchen stool where she sat. It seemed to say she was correct.

"Ah. I wonder. How does a ghost dog get trapped in a locket?"

There was a snuffle from below. She dusted her hands to remove toast crumbs.

"I don't suppose we'll ever find out. I don't suppose it matters."

Another snuffle.

"Well, Boo, I need to get a move on. Andrea will be back soon and I must tidy up."

***

Over the next few days, Caroline found herself becoming more and more attached to Boo. She was the perfect companion, sitting on Caroline's knee while she wrote, happily bumping around her ankles as she cooked and sitting outside the bathroom door, howling softly. Andrea seemed not to notice Caroline's new companion, she certainly never mentioned anything and Caroline was loathe to bring the matter up. But one thing was bothering Caroline. Someone had lost the locket, probably on the night Caroline had found it. Was that someone looking for it? Looking for Boo? Caroline felt bad. Was it moral to keep Boo without making the slightest effort to find her previous… owner? Caroline, who had been brought up properly by her mother and Uncle Fred, finally decided it wasn't. She would try to find the previous owner and if she couldn't, then she could keep both the locket and Boo in good conscience. She posted an announcement on various social media sites, as well as on the local Lost & Found website, and then she settled down to wait, with the sinking feeling she was about to say goodbye to her newfound friend.

A week passed and Caroline started to relax. She had honestly done her best to locate the previous owner of both the locket and the ghost. And then… then the email came through.

"Saw your message on SM. Sounds like the locket I lost on the same night. Happy to bring a photo of me wearing it. TTFN!"

"TTFN?" thought Caroline. She replied to the email.

The girl, the previous owner of the locket, was young and fashionable, wearing a blend of lace, high leather boots, a ruffled blouse, and antique jewelry. It was, Caroline knew, the outfit of choice for a particular group of twenty-somethings who mimicked the fashion of the Victorian era. She came accompanied by a doe-eyed boy, who smiled shyly. Caroline didn't invite them into the flat, instead leaving them in the hallway. The girl wasn't the person Caroline had imagined owning the locket, owning Boo. Caroline took the proffered phone and studied the photograph displayed on the screen. She recognised the locket hanging from the throat of the girl as she straddled herself across the laps of four young men. Clearly a character, Caroline surmised, choosing the worst insult invented by her mother to describe members of her own gender. Clearly a character. Caroline couldn't believe this person could care for Boo in the same way she could.

"I found the locket in the gutter on Canal Street."

"Oh yes, we went that way home from the tacky little bar on the corner down there. Used to be fashionable, now it's just ironic."

The bar referred to was where Caroline worked.

"Well, here it is," Caroline said, fishing it out from a pocket. She passed it over to the girl.

"Thank you so much. Having genuine jewelry from the period completes the ensemble, don't you think?"

Caroline just nodded.

"Well, thanks again. Bye!"

"Just one last thing."

"Yes?"

"How long have you owned her?"

"Her?"

Caroline felt her face flush.

"Sorry… it… the locket, I mean."

The girl looked as if she was about to laugh. Caroline hoped she wouldn't; she would either burst into tears or slap her. The girl managed to stifle her amusement.

"I had it for about two days before I lost it. I picked it up at the Flea Market on Johnson Street. Tarquin and I find some charming trinkets there, once in a while."

"Did you open it?"

"Open it? Of course, why wouldn't I? It might have contained a photograph or a lock of hair."

"I see. Well, goodbye!"

Caroline shut the door in their faces, leaning her face against the cool wood. Caroline, heart in her

81

mouth, called Boo. There was no response. As she had predicted, Boo had to go where the locket went, her spirit was bound to that earthly object. Caroline doubted the girl was even aware she had inherited a ghost when she opened the locket. She now wished she hadn't tried to find the owner; she had envisioned the person as someone who loved Boo just as much as she did, not some flighty young girl who couldn't possibly be aware of the little ghost dog following her around, day after day, waiting to be noticed. Waiting to be loved.

The rest of the day was spent in pyjamas and tears. Andrea read the signs correctly and left her alone, no doubt assuming man trouble or some other trivial disaster. As Caroline lay in bed, the sky turned from blue, to red and then to black. She switched on her bedside light, taking comfort in its warm glow. She wondered what colour fur Boo had. She opted for yellow, like a Labrador. The need for sleep pressed down onto her, she felt worn out, grieving for her little lost friend.

There was a scratch at the door. Her heart leapt. It couldn't be, could it? Caroline flung open the door and was nearly knocked over by the tiny furry body that jumped into her arms. There were tears again, but this time for a different reason. Boo was back. Caroline stroked her head.

"I missed you, Boo. I'm glad you came back. I just know that silly girl didn't even notice you."

A snuffle came from Boo, indicating agreement.

"Yes, too wrapped up in herself to see you. A silly ninny, as my old Uncle Fred used to say. You'll have to meet him one day. You might be able to see him."

Another snuffle and bump of a cold nose.

"And I'm glad you could free yourself from the locket. I wonder what allowed you to do that."

A tiny snuffle was the response. Caroline flushed red and tears pricked her eyes.

"Me?"

For the first and only time, Boo spoke.

"Woof."

A definite yes. A single tear ran down Caroline's cheek.

"It's been a long day. Time for bed."

Caroline settled into her warm bed, with Boo next to her. Then, just as she was drifting off, there was a scratching at her bedroom door. The noise brought her back to full consciousness, her hand immediately seeking Boo. Boo was there. So, what was at the door? She switched her bedside light on and went to open it. She had the sensation of a small furry creature timidly entering the room. A second set of indentations appeared on the duvet, next to the bump where Boo was sitting. Caroline had a feeling she knew what was going on.

"Boo, do you know anything about this?"

Despite Boo's invisibility, Caroline had the distinct impression the dog was looking guilty. She closed the door and walked over to the bed.

"Mm. I see, been spreading the word, have you, Boo? Come to Caroline, she'll look after us. Is that the message you've been passing around on your journey back here? I suppose there must be lots and lots of lost animals out there. Animals who can't find their way back home again."

She leaned in towards Boo, feeling breath on her face.

"You think I'm going to look after all these lost

spirits? Do you really?"

She smiled to herself.

"You know something, Boo, me old dear? You're absolutely flaming right!"

Boo jumped up and licked her face with joy. Caroline roared with laughter. She walked to the door of her bedroom, flung it wide open and shouted at the top of her voice, not caring if Andrea thought her insane.

"Everybody welcome! No one is turned away tonight!"

Still laughing she returned to her bed, feeling that this was absolutely the right thing to do. She couldn't wait to see what the morning would bring. Uncle Fred would be proud.

PRINCE OF PERSIAN

June Low

"WUH... WHERE AM I?"

I'm barely awake before a huge yawn overtakes me. When it passes, I blink back the tears and look around. I am on a very large bed. It is so wide the ground is impossible to see from where I am. Rolling onto my back, the ceiling soars high above my head. The purple and grey pattern on the bedspread looks vaguely familiar. This giant bed, this giant room, it all looks familiar. I've been here before. I bolt upright as I realize I've been here forever! The giant's castle! Memories of last night come flooding back. How she betrayed me with a promise. Left me on this giant bed. In this room, this prison cell! The door was slammed shut and locked. No hope of escape. Nothing I could do but wait for her return. I must have fallen asleep.

Curse this sleeping curse! It might have been longer than last night. I have to get out of here!

Moving to the edge of the bed, I peer over the side. The door of my prison now stands ajar. A most unexpected and suspicious development. I must proceed with caution. I listen, straining for any sound from my captor. The air is calm and dead silent. It looks like a two-story drop to the ground. I vault off the bed onto the floor, then pause. No one comes. I inch towards the doorway. Flattening myself against the door frame, I peek around the corner. The coast looks clear, and it is still completely silent. The giant's castle has been deserted overnight. This is not a good sign. I walk down the hallway, hugging the walls. I am still keeping alert but there seems to be no one else about.

I proceed further down the hallway when suddenly there is a loud flapping of wings. I shrink back into the shadows on the opposite wall and look in the direction of the sound. Through a large open doorway, giant windows look out to a blue sky. A grey speckled bird with a tiny beak and round eye just landed on a wire strung outside. It seems to be looking right at me, trying to tell me something.

Crossing the hallway, I enter the giant Library. Enormous bookcases line the wall, each filled with massive tomes and various artifacts. I walk up to the nearest one and mentally chart my route to the top, the closest point I can get to the bird. Bracing with my knees, I jump and grab on to the edge of the first shelf. I'm able to leap from shelf to shelf easily, despite the doodads that litter my path. Close to the top, I misjudge an attempt to squeeze past an interesting-looking thingamabob. My foot slips and knocks it off the shelf. It falls a long way and smashes onto the ground below me, bursting into a thousand glittering shards. I climb the last shelf and take a moment to catch my breath. The bird makes a "groo-groo" noise and slowly the sounds begin to form words.

"Keep up your strength. Find the way."

"How? The way to what?" I ask, standing up

against the window. When the bird does not respond, I shout and bang on the glass. "Do you mean the way out?" The bird appears unperturbed.

"Keep up your strength. Find the way," it repeats, without any change in tone or emotion. And with that, it hops around on the wire and flies away.

Stupid bird.

Disgusted, I jump down from the bookcase and leave the Library. The end of the hallway brings me to a giant flight of stairs. Flattening myself on my stomach, I slide up to the edge and look over. The stairs spiral downward, obscuring any view I might have of what lies below. My eyelids begin to droop. I'd better find a safe place before the curse takes hold of me again. Perhaps down there.

I descend the staircase and find myself having to squint against the flood of lights. This must be the Great Room. Immense glass-paneled doors lead out to a balcony beyond. Luxurious drapes hang from floor to ceiling on either side. Plush furnishings are arranged throughout. As I take in the enormous proportions of this room, the hairs on the back of my neck begin to prickle. A sinister presence is stalking me. Out of the corner of my eye, I see a ringed tail swish from behind a curtain. The lemur!

I race to the door and whip back the curtain, my daggers drawn. The giant lemur looks at me wide-eyed. Obviously it thought itself well hidden. I set upon it at once while I have the element of surprise. It lunges aside and hisses, baring its teeth.

"I thought I killed you!"

"As if it's that easy to kill a lemur!"

I feint left and thrust right. The lemur buys my feint and is caught off balance as I slam bodily against it, knocking it to the ground. We roll across the cold, hard floor as I struggle to keep its gouging fingers from my eyes. Then in a flash, it is gone. I cast quick glances about, but it seems to have vanished into thin air. I check myself for injuries, thankfully finding none. I will have to be careful from now on. I'm not as alone in the castle as I had thought.

I prowl a slow circle of the room, looking under furniture and around the potted plants. No sign of that darn lemur. I notice another bit of movement towards the middle of the room. The corner of a piece of paper flapping up in an ever so gentle breeze. Ah, the giant left one of her books! It lies open, spread out and inviting perusal. Perhaps this will provide some clues to what has transpired here. I lean in to read the large type on the top of the first page.

"A cuticle in the space station."

What? That makes no sense. I scan further down the page and find another line.

"Borage makes new jam gains."

Furrowing my brow, I squint at the text. The sentence changes before my eyes.

"Ultimate daytime for gypsum lane."

What sorcery is this? I turn the page, skimming the black text but the words appear to swim before my eyes. Frantically, I turn page after page, searching for something, anything that makes some sense. The desperation causes me to shake and grip too hard, ripping the thin paper to shreds. Soon, there is nothing left but a pile of finely shredded bits of black and white. Exhausted, I give myself over to the sleep that has been repeatedly dogging me.

I feel refreshed when I awake what feels like only moments later. There are whiffs of a delicious aroma wafting towards me. I follow the smell into the main kitchen. There is a large bowl on the floor. It is overflowing with food. Remembering the words of the grey speckled bird, my stomach begins to growl. I have to eat to keep up my strength. But what if it is a trap? The growling in my stomach grows more insistent.

I put my nose low to the bowl and inhale deeply. It doesn't smell foul. I select a morsel and eat it. Feeling no ill effects after a few moments, I decide it is probably safe to consume. I am careful to only eat from the middle, because if food is poisoned, it would be around the edges. I must be careful to stay away from the rim.

I am cleaning up after the meal when my stomach begins to sour. Damn! It must have been poisoned! I dash out of the kitchen, down the hallway towards the Great Room. One of the plants there I'd recognized earlier as an emetic. It might not be too late to make myself eject the poison.

The plant is perched on a high platform on a single spindly column. I can almost reach a leaf. The pot begins to teeter and tip over. I jump out of the way just in time as the heavy planter comes crashing over the edge. And then I hear that sinister hissing laugh. The lemur leans over the edge, grinning its wide tooth-filled grin.

"You again!" I snarl.

"Banzai!"

The lemur makes a flying leap off the top of the platform. Daggers at the ready, I brace for the impact. At the last moment, it twists and flips over my head, landing behind me. I swivel around but it grabs me in a bear hug. Reaching behind me, I wrench as hard as I can, pulling it off my back. It wriggles out of my grasp, the slippery fiend. I run towards the fallen plant, reaching out to seize two leaves. The waxy fronds slip through my grasp just as my feet are yanked out from under me. Twisting onto my back, I kick out hard, dislodging its grabby hands from around my ankles. Scrambling to my feet, I pounce, knocking it to the ground. Springing onto its chest, I press all my weight through my knees. I grab around its neck and wring with all my might. The lemur reaches for me ineffectually and I feel its grip weaken within seconds. Its eyes roll back in its head and its tongue begins to protrude grotesquely from its open mouth. I roll off its limp form, breathing a deep sigh of relief.

I go over to the fallen plant and gather a couple of leaves. Cramming them into my mouth, I chew furiously. Ignoring the bitter taste, I force myself to swallow. The effects are almost immediate. Already, I feel the wave of nausea rise up from my stomach to the back of my throat. I gag and gag again. I'm on all fours, unable to hold my head up as the convulsions grow stronger. I heave onto the floor a small mountain of undigested food.

"Ugh."

I move away from the mess, feeling slightly better but weakened. So much for keeping up my strength. My eyes won't stay open as the curse easily catches up with me. I crawl under an enormous sofa in the corner. This should keep me hidden from that lemur's friends while I catch a quick nap.

A sudden noise jars me awake. It is a mixed sound, clinking and rattling and even a muffled voice. I'm immediately alert. The sound seems to be coming from outside the Great Room. Scrambling out from under the sofa, I rush across the Great Room to an enormous door. Staring up at it, it must be twenty beings tall. How had I not seen this before? The ornate knob halfway up the massive wooden panel is rattling, as if some giant on the other side were attempting to dismantle it.

I cast a quick glance left and right. There is nowhere to hide. Every muscle in my body tenses as I prepare for the inevitable.

***

Sophie pushed the door open slowly, expecting a little grey striped head to come poking through the opening. She smiled down at the tabby cat sniffing at the tips of her shoes.

"Why, hello there, Aubrey. Did you miss me, kitty-kins?"

She pushed the door open wider to let herself in, blocking the opening with her body and gently forcing the cat to step back into the entryway.

"Did you have awesome adventures while I was gone?" She crouched down to scratch between its ears. Instantly, she was rewarded with the low "rrr-rrr" rumble of a purr. The cat pushed his fuzzy head against her hand, then past it to rub against her legs as she straightened up and surveyed the living room.

The potted plant on the corner side table had been overturned onto the floor, dirt from the pot scattered around it, the leaves chewed up. Last Friday's newspaper lay in shreds on the carpet next to the tattered soft toy lemur. Close by was a small pile of cat vomit. Aubrey arched his back against Sophie's shins, purring. He brushed insistently against the bottoms of her jeans, leaving a mat of white hairs on them.

"I guess that's the last time I go away for a

weekend," Sophie grumbled to herself.

Aubrey looked up at her with green eyes and let out a big yawn. "Mrreow?"

A DOG CALLED ALFRED

Ginny Swart

KATHERINE EVANS walked slowly down the row of cages at the animal shelter, each one containing three or four dogs. Some leapt up against the mesh, their tails whipping into a frenzy as they yelped, others treated her approach with more dignity and simply gave her a welcoming thump of their tails without getting up.

All of them were appealing in their own way and all of them needed what Miss Burrows behind the desk called a forever home.

Forever is a myth, thought Katherine, who was in two minds about adopting a dog at all. Her neighbor Ellen, who had two corgis of her own, had encouraged her, telling her she was lonely in that big empty house. Telling her she needed an animal to care for. Someone to come home to.

Now that James has left you, she hadn't said, but that was what she'd meant.

James' leaving had been very much a mutual decision but she hadn't felt she had to explain everything to Ellen.

Suddenly she couldn't face the thought of taking

home a dog. Making such a lengthy commitment to an animal she wasn't even sure she wanted would be a mistake, for herself and the dog.

Katherine muttered something apologetic to Miss Burrows and was about to leave when the woman called after her.

"I suppose you wouldn't be interested in offering a dog a temporary home just for a month or so? We have a beautiful big boy who needs a foster mummy!"

Foster mummy. Katherine almost laughed but then thought, only one month? I could do that. A sort of trial run to test the water, to see if I really want a dog.

"Let me see him," she said cautiously.

"He's in the last kennel on the right, number 17."

She retraced her steps and stood outside the cage. At first it appeared to house a pile of rough black fur, then it turned into an enormous dog which raised his head from his paws and looked at her. He rose slowly, with great dignity and walked over to the mesh, bestowing a sniff of approval on her outstretched hand, then sat back and gazed at her steadily, as though awaiting her decision.

Katherine gazed into his deep brown eyes under the thatch of eyebrows and felt an immediate connection.

"Poor boy," she thought. "You're lonely, aren't you? I know the feeling."

He was a great deal bigger than any dog she'd planned to adopt, and his long matted coat meant he would be high-maintenance. She'd pictured a small, smooth-haired dog which wouldn't take up much space. This dog had a large, noble head and an air of calm and authority and would probably take up as much of her home as she'd allow.

Katherine pushed her hand through the mesh and scratched him under his bearded chin and he lifted his head to accept this caress. He seemed to be smiling. She knew she had found her dog.

"You'll take him? That's wonderful. As I said, he's just looking for a home for a month or two. His owner's in hospital and can't give him proper care and attention for a while. But as you can see, he's a big dog and he'll need a lot of exercise. A long walk every day."

"I enjoy a good walk, it's just what I need," she said. "And I live on the edge of town with open fields very near me."

The paper formalities complete, and the inspector sent to approve her canine accommodation, she drove home the following day with the black dog filling most of the back seat. Katherine realized she'd forgotten to ask his name.

"You need a name, don't you boy?" she murmured. "You should be called something serious and dignified. What if your name was Buster? That would be ridiculous."

Alfred. That had a noble ring to it. Alfred, Lord Tennyson.

"Alfred?" she said out loud and he cocked his ears slightly. "What d'you think, boy?"

He sighed deeply and pressed his hairy chin against her shoulder, tickling her neck. She reached back and scratched his head. Alfred it was.

Alfred fitted in with very little fuss. He toured her small garden, staking his claim at every point, then came inside and politely finished off the kibble she had bought. Katherine found an old blanket and laid it on the floor in a corner of the kitchen but after inspection, he decided the old sofa in the living room suited him better. He hopped up and stretched out, his back legs dangling over the edge and his head comfortably on the cushion at the other end.

"You're just lucky I've been planning to have that recovered," she muttered. "As soon as you've gone back home, that's what I'll do."

But she couldn't help smiling at the sight of him asleep. She took out her sketchbook and drew a quick line drawing of him. It had been some time since she'd picked up her charcoal, she realized. Not since before James had left. It felt good to get a picture down on paper again and Alfred was the ideal subject, lying perfectly still with his shaggy coat and ungainly long legs stuck out in front of him. Even asleep his expression was one of benign amusement.

The following day she clipped on his leash and walked him to the fields a short distance away, then let him free to run. He shot off, and she burst out laughing to see him leaping into the air like a springbok and bounding in circles like a puppy, all dignity forgotten.

"Morning. That's a fine big dog." A man walking a cocker spaniel stopped to admire Alfred. "What breed is he?"

"I don't know," she confessed. "I'm just looking after him for a friend."

Alfred stopped leaping about and rejoined Katherine, moving closer to her, almost as if he were guarding her. She stroked his ears in recognition of this fealty.

"There could be a bit of Briard in there," he said, considering. "And Great Dane? Whatever he is, I expect he takes a lot of feeding."

"You're right, he does eat a lot." Katherine knew she was going to have to buy a larger bag of kibble to last the month. And some big bones. And a heavy-duty dog brush.

They walked for about an hour across the fields and into the little wood which ran along the border. She found herself talking to Alfred, pointing out the butterflies and commenting on the birds she spotted. It was almost as though she was walking with James, except that James had never been interested in butterflies or birds and his only responses had been a grunt. And towards the end he'd walked in stony silence.

Back home, Alfred stretched out on the sofa to recover from his exertions but Katherine felt wonderfully refreshed and headed to the garden to do some weeding. She'd forgotten how good she felt after a nice long walk. Later that evening after tea, she and Alfred watched television, he on the sofa and she on her easy chair. She could have sworn he watched the animal programme with genuine interest although she knew this wasn't likely.

They eased into a pleasant routine of daily afternoon walks, varying their routes to explore the fields farther away. Katherine replaced his old brown collar with one of smart red leather and had a disc engraved for it with her name and her phone number on it, in case he got lost. But he was never far from her side. He walked with her to the shops and she became used to dealing with exclamations about his size and accepting the compliments about his glossy coat. Brushing every night had changed him from a pile of matted black wool to a shining, although still very hairy, man-about-town.

Katherine's life started to pick up again after what felt like a long hibernation. She began to paint once

97

more, something she'd abandoned a few years before, and realized how much she'd missed it.

A few weeks later her neighbor Ellen knocked briefly on the front door and sailed right in.

Alfred ambled to the door and flapped his tail in a dignified greeting.

"Good heavens!" she said, eyeing him. "And who are *you?*"

"This is Alfred," said Katherine, feeling proprietal. "Isn't he lovely?"

"I thought you were going to get a *small* dog," said Ellen, dubiously. "Not this huge hairy mutt."

"He's a bit hairy but he's no mutt," said Katherine firmly. "He's very intelligent. Anyway, he's sort of boarding with me. His owner is in hospital and when she can cope with him again, he'll go home."

"He must cost a fortune to feed?"

"Not really. But I don't mind, he's a real companion. You were right, Ellen, a dog was just what I needed. One like Alfred."

"Well, you're looking really good. A lot more cheerful than last time I saw you. How's your teapot?"

Ellen went through to the kitchen and chatted while Katherine made the tea and when they went to the living room, she gave a little cry of delight.

"You've started painting again! Katherine, these are beautiful."

Katherine had painted two pictures of Alfred, one of him gamboling in the field full of daisies and the other a portrait with him looking straight at her.

She was particularly proud of that one. Usually people who did animal studies worked from photographs but Alfred had been the perfect model. Whenever she asked him to, he'd sat quite still and gazed at her from under his bushy eyebrows and she felt she'd caught his gentle expression and the quizzical look in his eye.

"Do you like it? I do too, it's one of my best."

"You should enter that in the art exhibition at the community hall," said Ellen immediately. "Honestly, it looks so professional. And exactly like Alfred too. You're so clever."

"Do you think so? James always said I wasn't nearly ready to exhibit."

"Oh well, *James.*" Ellen dismissed him. "He just held you back because he was jealous of your talent. You really must enter it. If you don't, I'll come and snatch it off your wall and enter it for you!"

"And you probably would, too! All right, you've persuaded me." Katherine smiled. "I'll find out how to go about it."

She'd never exhibited any of her work, mainly, she realized, because James had not encouraged her to try. The longer she lived without him, the more she realized what a dampening effect he had had on her. She took both paintings up to the community hall the following day and entered them.

"What are the titles?" asked the girl behind the desk.

"I didn't know I needed a title. Well, maybe this one could be "Dog Amongst the Daisies?""

"Perfect," said the girl, writing it out on her list. "And this one? My, isn't he a beautiful animal!"

"He is. Just call that one Alfred," said Katherine.

***

The following Sunday she was unprepared for the

evening phone call from the headmistress.

"Katherine, I know you're only one term away from retirement," said Mrs. Hammond. "But I've been asked to send an observer to the teacher's conference in Brighton starting tomorrow and Margaret was going, but now she has flu and I thought, seeing you haven't any family to make arrangements for..."

"How long is this conference?" she asked warily.

"Five days. All expenses paid and you get to stay in that nice hotel on the beachfront. You'll enjoy it."

Katherine very much doubted it, but she unwillingly agreed. At the end of term she'd walk out of the school door forever, after thirty-seven years. She couldn't wait.

But what to do with Alfred? There was nothing for it but to return him to the kennels for the week, and explain the situation to Miss Burrows.

"I'll probably be away about six days," she said the following morning. "But I'll phone you as soon as I get back and collect him again."

"No need," said Miss Burrows breezily. "Major Anderson let me know yesterday that he is able to take his dog home again this weekend. I was going to call you today."

"Oh no!" Katherine was taken aback. "So this is goodbye, my dear Alfred." She stroked his head and Miss Burrows started to lead him away.

"My, what a smart new collar you've bought him," she commented. "I'm sure Major Anderson will want to phone you and thank you for your kindness. He's looking beautiful."

"Yes, isn't he," said Katherine hollowly. Was this the last time she'd see Alfred?

She stayed in Brighton for the five days, listening

with half an ear to the delegates and making desultory notes. But she wished she had brought her painting things and by the time she boarded the train home she was itching to take out her paints and start again.

Her house seemed very quiet and empty without Alfred to welcome her with his throaty woof, his long bushy tail waving gently. I wonder how he's doing back with that Major Anderson, she thought sadly. Anyone who could allow their dog to get into such a state as Alfred had been, didn't deserve to have a dog at all, in her opinion. Although perhaps the man had been too ill to look after him properly?

Katherine walked from one room to the other, unable to settle. Alfred's water bowl was still in the kitchen and the sight of it brought a lump to her throat. No more Alfred. No more gentle thumps of his tail when she entered the room, no more enthusiastic walks with him bounding ahead. She recognized a long-forgotten feeling. Loneliness.

She had hardly been back an hour when Ellen phoned.

"I've just been up to the art exhibition and I see both your paintings have been sold," she said. "Congratulations!"

"Sold? Oh my goodness, I didn't really think anyone would buy them. I gave them each a ridiculous price because I didn't really want to sell them at all."

"Well, they both have red stickers on their frames," said Ellen. "And I'm not surprised, they are really good, Katherine."

Katherine took herself up to the community hall the following day, the last day of the exhibition. She picked up a catalogue and walked over to where her two studies of Alfred were hanging together. She looked at them judiciously. Ellen was right, they are good, she thought, but the sight of the red stickers dismayed her. She'd counted on having at least the memory of Alfred on her walls, and she knew she could never paint these again without him to pose for her.

"Beautiful, aren't they?" The man's voice at her shoulder startled her. "And they're mine! Aren't I lucky."

She turned to see a tall thin man leaning heavily on a cane, smiling at her.

"You bought these? So, you're a dog lover?"

"Well, I am, but that's my dog, Fred. The artist caught a perfect likeness, it's amazing."

So this was Major Anderson.

"I'm the artist," she said quietly. "I painted him. And I've been looking after him for the past two months."

"You're *Katherine Evans*? Good heavens. Fred's angel in disguise! I've been trying to phone you for a week, to thank you. I found your telephone number on his collar."

"I've been away," she said. "But it was a pleasure looking after him, it really was. And by some odd coincidence, I called him Alfred. After Alfred, Lord Tennyson. I thought it was a noble name to suit him."

"And I called him Alfred, after Alfred the Great because I knew he was going to grow into a big dog. But he was such a clown when he was a pup that he turned into Fred pretty quickly, I'm afraid."

She smiled and was about to move away politely when she couldn't help adding, "Now he's home with you I hope you're going to brush him more often." She tried not to sound too severe. "I realize he's a very high-maintenance dog. But he's so lovely when he's brushed."

"I know he is. I don't know what you must have thought of me when you saw him at the shelter. Won't you let me buy you coffee and tell you his history? Well, our history I suppose."

The note of diffident appeal in his voice caught her by surprise.

"Of course I will. Thank you."

He led the way to the little café next to the community hall, leaning awkwardly on his stick. They ordered coffee and sat in silence for a moment. Katherine studied him. There were lines of strength and humour in his face there but it was gaunt and pale, with speckles of recently healed scar tissue under the thinning grey hair. A quiet man, bookish, she thought. He didn't look at all like a soldier.

"I've been in the army all my life so having a dog wasn't really an option. Being sent to various parts of the world for months at a time didn't leave me much time for a settled home life. But I thought my last tour of duty in Afghanistan was going to be my final and I was all set to be in the office at HQ until I retired. A nine-to-five for the first time in my life."

"That must have been quite a change for you."

"A good one. And it meant I could adopt Fred when he was a pup. He came from the animal shelter," he said. "No one knew his exact parentage, all they could tell me was his mother had been a Great Dane and that he'd grow to be a very big dog."

"They were right," said Katherine with a smile.

"But I'd had him for about a year when unfortunately someone remembered I could speak Farsi." He gave a wry smile.

"Farsi! Good heavens."

"And Arabic. And Kurdish. And a smattering of Urdu. They needed me to translate and I was deployed to Afghanistan again. By this time Fred was almost fully-grown. I had to find a temporary home for him and because of his size there weren't many takers."

"I can imagine," murmured Katherine.

"It was tough to leave him. I'd lived alone for a long time and I'd grown to be really fond of the big mutt, if you know what I mean. He's a pretty special dog, a real companion."

"I do know what you mean," said Katherine softly. It was clear that Major Anderson really loved Alfred. It hadn't been his fault that his coat had been such a mess.

"Well in the end my younger brother agreed to keep him but it wasn't ideal. He lived in a small townhouse with a garden the size of a flag. And he worked in IT and kept odd hours so poor Alfred never got taken for proper walks and really, I think Kevin just fed him. But it was only supposed to be a six month call-up and I hoped he would manage until I got back. But then my tour of duty was extended and at the same time Kevin got a job in America so he passed poor Alfred on to my mum, who really wasn't able to look after such a big dog in her little flat."

"Poor Alfred."

"And then I ran into a spot of bother in Helmand and I was shipped home three months ago, a bit the worse for wear. Mum did her best but then the caretaker of her block told her she couldn't keep such a big dog and she had to ask the shelter to look after him until I was well enough to leave hospital."

"And now you are." A spot of bother? She wondered what horrors this quiet understatement covered.

"Well, yes. Now I am, more or less. And I'm delighted to have Fred back and looking so wonderful. All thanks to you." His face warmed into a fond smile. "And he remembered me, I could see. He didn't stop wagging his tail, although of course he's a lot quieter than he used to be. I suppose he's grown up."

"Not when he's on his walks! But how do you manage for those?" she asked.

"Not too well, I'm afraid. For the next six weeks I have to spend every morning having physiotherapy on my legs." He cleared his throat. "I might have to employ a dog walker until I'm rid of this wretched stick. If I can find someone with enough energy."

Along with the hopeful look she detected a mischievous twinkle in his eye.

"There's always me," she said hesitantly. "He and I have been doing an hour across the fields most days. I'd love to carry on walking with him."

"Really? You wouldn't mind?" His cheerful relief made her suspect he'd been hoping for her offer.

"Not at all." Then she had a sudden inspiration. "Maybe it would be easier if he could sort of board with me during the week and then go home to you on the weekends?"

I hope that doesn't sound too devious, she thought, surprised at herself. But she suddenly wanted to know this man better and that way, she'd see him at least twice a week.

"It's a deal." He leaned across the table and shook her hand. "By the way, if we're going to have joint ownership for a while, I'd better introduce myself. I'm Michael Anderson."

"Hello, Michael," she smiled.

"Perhaps I could join the two of you for a short part

105

of the walk as my leg gets stronger?"

"I'd like that very much," she said.

They smiled at each other, pleased with what they saw.

And later, she decided, she'd ask if he'd sit for a portrait of himself. With Alfred, of course.

DOG DAY

Michael Penncavage

EVELYN CRABTREE WAS sitting down with her afternoon tea to watch her favorite soap opera when she heard the unmistakable clicking of nails on the wood floor above her.

She placed her tea down onto the doily, picked up the phone, and dialed. It rang twice.

"Hello?"

"Leonard, do you have a dog up there?"

"How are you doing, Evelyn?" he answered in his normal cheery voice.

She hated young tenants. Always bubbly. If Leonard hadn't been so timely with the rent checks, she never would have let him extend the lease.

"I heard the nails tapping on the wood, Leonard. On the lease it specifically states that no pets are allowed." Leonard was silent on the other end. She felt victorious. Leonard always played his music loud and it was always an issue with him to lower it. Each time she spoke to him about it, Evelyn felt like she was compromising.

There would be no compromise this time.

"He's really a good dog, Evelyn. I found him over at the dump. I think he might have been exposed to something there because he really is smart—"

"I don't care, Leonard!" she snapped back at him. Evelyn shuddered to think what types of bugs and diseases the animal had contracted at the dump. "You have until tomorrow to bring it to the pound."

"If I bring him to the pound, they are just going to put him to sleep," Leonard replied in a slightly louder voice.

Evelyn then found herself talking to the dial tone. *I'll give that boy until noon tomorrow.* She picked up her tea. It had grown cold. She put it back down in disgust, and clicked the television on.

***

The program was just ending when she heard Leonard leave the house. Peering through the blinds, she saw him walk to his car, alone.

Above her, she could hear the nails making that infernal noise. *If that thing pisses on the carpet, he's not going to get his security deposit back.*

Getting up, she went into the kitchen to fix herself a fresh cup of tea. As the kettle was beginning to tweet, she heard the faint sound of water trickling down the pipes inside the wall. The toilet had been flushed. She silenced the kettle, and heard the click, click, click again.

Evelyn stared at the ceiling, and followed the noise until she was in her dining room. Above her was the kitchen. Again, she began to hear the faint trickling of water. Someone was using the kitchen sink.

A frown appeared on her face. *So, he had someone*

living up there as well. It stated in the lease that Leonard could not sublet any of the apartment.

The ceiling started to vibrate. The radio had been turned on. The music was playing so loud that Evelyn could tell which Bruce Springsteen song it was. "Born in the USA." She watched as a picture of her late husband, Earl, began shaking on the wall.

She dialed up the apartment. The phone rang but no one picked it up. Slamming the phone back onto the receiver, she tried to keep her anger under control. Her doctor warned about her high blood pressure. There was no doubt that this wasn't helping.

She tried calling again, but to no avail. Bruce had now given way to Billy Joel.

Grabbing the spare set of keys, she strode out of the house and around the side to Leonard's entrance.

She banged on the door and rang the bell. No one answered. Even from outside, she could hear the thump, thump, thump of the bass.

She gripped the keys, unlocked the door, and went inside.

The stairs wound up, then left, and she entered the small vestibule-like room.

"Hello!" she shouted but her voice was drowned out by the music. Evelyn walked into the living room and turned off the stereo. "Is anyone here?"

She heard the clicking again and a dog emerged from the kitchen. If not for the blackish tail, she would have thought it a purebred golden retriever. The dog looked clean and well groomed. *Probably hiding some sort of junkyard disease.*

"Sit," she commanded. Immediately, the dog sat down.

"Lie down." The dog placed his chin between his

paws.

"Play dead." The dog rolled onto his back and stuck his paws up in the air.

Leonard was right— the dog was well trained.

Evelyn began walking through the apartment. She went into each room, looked in every closet, and even peered under the bed. She checked the windows, but they were all fastened shut. All the while, the dog followed behind her, his tongue hanging out the side of his mouth like a slice of baloney.

Back in the vestibule, Evelyn placed her hands on her hips in frustration. *Where was the person hiding?*

A beep sounded in the kitchen. Her curiosity piqued, she walked towards it. The kitchen was the only room she had not searched.

The microwave had gone off. A familiar scent emanated from it. She opened the door and found a hot bag of popcorn. She took it out, ripped the bag open and popped several kernels into her mouth. *Ah, nice and warm. Just how she liked it.* It did have a peculiar taste that Evelyn simply dismissed as a new flavor.

Evelyn heard the click, click, click again. The dog came into view. He looked at her and growled. Evelyn was taken back by this behavior.

"Scram!" she yelled, but the dog didn't move.

"Move it!"

The dog bared its teeth and growled again.

Evelyn's temper flared. She placed the bag down and looked underneath the sink. After taking out a bottle of floor cleaner, she walked over to the dog's water bowl. She poured a capful into the water. She put the bottle back and grabbed the popcorn.

The dog had left the kitchen. She was curious if the dog had seen her do it. Not that it really mattered. She walked back downstairs, eating another handful of popcorn.

She was certainly going to give Leonard an earful when he came home.

***

From the bedroom window, the dog watched as Evelyn walked outside and back into her apartment. He closed the shade, and went back into the kitchen. From the pantry he pulled out a fresh package of popcorn. After setting the microwave for three minutes on high, the dog then took the water bowl and dumped the contents into the sink. Once he was sure it was fully rinsed, he filled it back up with fresh water. *Stupid woman. Even if she put the cleaner in when I wasn't looking, it was easy enough to smell. If you're going to poison someone, you have to use something harder to detect. Like rat poison. Rat poison was easy to mix with the food such as popcorn.*

He took out a bottle of Bud from the refrigerator, and used the counter's edge to pop the cap off. It made a deep scrape in the finish.

He walked to the living room and turned the stereo back on. "Amanda" by Boston was playing. Not his favorite song, but it would do. Placing a paw on the knob marked volume, he raised it up. The bass was set so high that it began rattling one of the nearby window panes.

Not that it really mattered.

He didn't expect anyone to call complaining.

SCHRODINGER'S OTHER CAT

Laurie Axinn Gienapp

In the mid-1930's, Austrian physicist Erwin Schrodinger developed a thought experiment, a paradox, known as Schrodinger's Cat. There was no actual experiment, and it is unknown whether Schrodinger ever owned a cat. But if he did...

DAPHNE STRETCHED AND yawned, and tried to decide if she was hungry. After a moment she concluded that she was enjoying the sunshine too much to leave her spot. The sunshine typically disappeared far too soon, whereas her food bowl was always full. Or at least almost always. Occasionally the man would forget, but a few loud meows were generally enough to jog his memory.

Some time later, she woke up again. The sun had moved, and there was no longer a comfortable place in the warmth of the rays. Daphne had long since stopped trying to figure out where or why it went, and eventually the sunshine always came back. She got up and strolled over to her food dish, only to conclude she wasn't hungry after all. She moved to her water dish, put her paw in, and splashed water over the edge, watching it run along the floor.

"Daphne! How many times do I have to tell you to quit playing in your water?" the man asked.

Daphne looked up at the man and blinked. He always seemed to think it was cute when she blinked. Even if she had been able to talk, she certainly wasn't going to tell him that no matter how many times he told her to quit, if she was bored, she was going to play in her water. She blinked again.

"Aw Daphne, you are so cute." The man picked her up and scratched under her chin. She liked when he scratched under her chin. She would have rewarded him with a purr, but she didn't feel like being held right now, so she jumped down. She considered splashing some more water, but changed her mind. Overall, she did like the man and the things he did for her, so she rubbed against his leg and then sauntered over to the couch. She jumped up, pulled the afghan down from the back of the couch, and after several minutes of kneading it and making it soft, she curled into a circle on top of the afghan and went back to sleep.

The next time she woke up, she heard the man talking. She looked over, and saw him holding that thing he called a phone up to his ear.

"I'm telling you, Werner," she heard the man say, "it's a dilemma. There's just no answer for it in quantum—" Clearly this didn't involve her, so Daphne quit listening.

She jumped off the couch and strolled over to the fireplace and looked up. Often she did this even when nothing was there, merely to amuse the man. Or maybe it annoyed him. She wasn't quite sure. But as it happened, this time she did see something. She saw a dust mote slowly drifting down from the ceiling. She followed its downward progress for a moment, and then looked back up to see if there were any more.

She heard the man chuckle. He still had the phone thing held against his ear.

"Werner, you should see Daphne. She's doing that thing again where she pretends she sees something, and she's staring as hard as she can at a spot. And of course there's nothing there."

Daphne didn't correct him, but she did decide that maybe there was nothing more coming down from the ceiling, so she began to wash her face.

Suddenly, she perked up her ears. She thought she'd heard the man say something about a cat. Except that he usually called her Daphne, not cat. Was there another cat? She wasn't sure how she felt about that. When she'd first come to live with the man, there had been another cat. It was an old cat. And before she and the other cat could figure out whether they liked each other or not, the other cat died. Which was sad. But on the other hand, it meant the man gave all of his attention to her. Then the man had brought a gerbil into the house. She'd definitely liked the gerbil, but the man had been very loud and noisy with her when he'd realized she'd eaten it. That had been somewhat of a surprise. Not only had it never occurred to her that maybe she wasn't supposed to eat it, but she still had no idea why the man would bring a rodent home if it wasn't intended as a special treat for her. In any event, the man hadn't brought home anything else that was alive, since then. But he did bring toys and catnip, and that was good.

Wait! What was that? She needed to pay attention,

because she thought she heard the word cat again.

"I'm telling you, Werner. The theory is very simple. Podolsky has no idea what he's talking about. Let's say I put the cat in the box, and close up the box. And I put in a cartridge. And the cartridge is set to open at a random time."

Daphne quit listening as she started thinking about the cat that the man had put in a box. She hadn't noticed a box in the apartment, but she didn't bother paying attention to things that didn't matter to her. Perhaps she needed to give the apartment a thorough scan. Fortunately the place wasn't very big. She went to the bathroom first. She knew that this was where the man "did his business," and while she was horrified at the idea of doing one's bodily functions inside the building, at least he did a fair job of keeping the room clean.

After she jumped into the bathtub and back out, and then checked at the back of the toilet, she was sure that there was no new box in the bathroom. And she was pretty sure that there was no other cat, as well. She pawed at a drawer and managed to open it, but then decided to not climb in. She'd done that one time, and hadn't been able to get back out. But she did sniff around and was pretty sure that there was no cat in there anyway.

Daphne moved on to the bedroom. She jumped on the bed and stalked across the pillow, but found nothing there. She decided to practice her pouncing, and pounced on the bottom left corner of the bed. Yes! If something had been there, she would most certainly have gotten it. She jumped down and crawled under the bed. Finding a stuffed mouse that she'd left there last week, she batted it about for a moment, and then left it there for tomorrow. Daphne came back out from under the bed and leapt onto the dresser. There was no box there and no signs of another cat, but she saw some shiny cufflinks and batted them to the floor. Jumping back down, she made her way around the dresser and then nosed her way into the closet. She made note of a really interesting-smelling sock in the bottom of the closet, but she didn't see a box or another cat.

Daphne went to the kitchen next, because now she was hungry. She sniffed at her food bowl, and was pleased to discover that it was the same kind of food she had yesterday. For some reason, the man kept changing her food. She didn't really see the point. If she liked the food one day, she'd like it the next day. Probably. Most of the time she'd eat what he set out. But every now and then, especially if he was watching her, she'd paw at the food as if she was outside, covering up, mostly because his reaction was so amusing.

Daphne finished crunching her third piece of food, and was ready to move on. Or to nap. She stood there trying to make up her mind, when she heard the phone thing make that loud noise.

"Schrodinger, here... Oh hello, Niels. Werner Heisenberg and I were just talking about that, and your name came up. Are you still in Copenhagen?... Well then, you and Werner should come over tonight."

Daphne let out a small purr of pleasure. While she wasn't quite sure who the man was talking to, or who he was talking about, she got the sense that people would be coming over. For the most part, she liked the man's friends. They generally made a fuss over her, and some of them brought her treats. She certainly wanted to look her best when they arrived, so she began washing her face, paying particular attention to her ears and her tail. When she finished, Daphne decided she had earned a nap. She wandered into the bedroom and jumped up on the bed. Noticing a disruption in the covers on the bottom left corner of the bed, she pounced on it, but there was nothing there. Even so, she went to the opposite corner of the bed and curled up on the pillow.

Daphne was awakened by a vaguely familiar voice. It didn't belong to the man, but she felt she'd heard it before.

"Yes, I see her, Erwin. I will admit that she is cute, although I don't know that I would want a cat on my pillow."

Daphne wondered what was wrong with the man's friend, or why someone wouldn't want a cat on their pillow. The friend approached and Daphne considered attacking him, but then he rubbed her ears so she forgave him. There was a knock on the door and both the man and his friend left the bedroom, and Daphne thought perhaps she should attack whoever had so rudely interrupted the ear rubbing she'd been enjoying. While she had enjoyed it when the friend rubbed her ears, it had created an itch. She stopped to scratch the itch and was going to return to her nap, when she heard voices in the living room. Oh, right, maybe someone would bring her a treat.

She washed her face once again, and then meandered into the living room. There were three humans sitting on the furniture, but none of them noticed her. She went over to the man and rubbed against his leg. He reached down to pet her, but that was all. She was going to walk over to the Erwin friend, but decided she didn't want her ears to itch again. So she walked over to the other friend—she thought this might be the one the man called Niels—and rubbed against him, but he was moving his hands in the air and he ignored her.

Daphne stopped and watched his hands a moment, but decided that was boring. Oh. Boring. Maybe she'd head over to her water dish and splash in the water and watch it run down the sides of the bowl. She walked into the kitchen, making sure to keep her tail up in the air, so that the man and his friends would know they had displeased her. She got to her water dish and decided to take a drink. She had just dipped her head to the bowl when she heard one of the friends laugh and say "We could call it Schrodinger's cat."

While she was delighted that they were thinking of her, she was surprised to hear this. She wasn't anyone's cat, she just let the man take care of her. And then she heard the man say "That's what I told Werner. The cat is in the box—" And suddenly Daphne remembered. She was looking for some box with another cat in it.

She sat down and tried to recall where she'd looked for the box. Or was she looking for the cat? She concluded she must be looking for both. She looked around, and then also up at the ceiling, just in case. But there was nothing in here that looked suspicious. Or interesting. Daphne decided maybe she had better explore the entryway next. The entryway wasn't very big, so she checked every corner, carefully. She didn't know how large this box or this cat was supposed to be. She was nearly done, when she noticed that the hall closet wasn't shut tight. Maybe that would be a good place to hide a box. Or a cat.

Using her paw, she was able to pull the door open a bit more. She stood with her face near the opening, testing it with her whiskers. After a moment, she felt sure that she could fit through without difficulty. It was dark in the closet, which made it easier to see movement. Daphne stood still for a moment and decided nothing was moving. But the box might still be in here, and maybe there was a cat inside.

She sniffed at a pair of shoes, and then raised up on her hind legs and sniffed at the bottom of a long wool coat. Neither seemed worthy of further attention.

And then she saw a shoebox in the corner of the closet. That was a box. And shoeboxes were good for cats. This shoebox didn't have a lid on it, but she couldn't quite see inside from where she was standing. Carefully weaving her way through the shoes and boots, she approached the box and peered inside. She didn't see a cat, although there was a crumpled piece of tissue paper in the box. She didn't smell a cat, but you could never be too careful. There was that old saying, better to pounce than be pounced upon. So she hunkered down, shook out her muscles to loosen them up, and leapt into the box onto the ball of tissue paper. The box skidded a short distance as a result of her jump, but that didn't matter. She held the tissue paper between her paws and confirmed that nothing was hiding inside.

"Erwin! What was that noise?"

"It sounded like it came from the coat closet. Did one of you gentlemen decide to play a trick on me?"

"It wasn't me. Werner, did you do something?"

"No. Maybe you have a mouse, Erwin."

Schrodinger laughed. "With Daphne around? I don't think so. One of these days I'll tell you what happened when I brought a pet gerbil home."

"There was definitely a noise. I think you need to

119

check it out."

"Niels, you have always been on the timid side. It's probably just the cat playing around. Fine, fine. I'll take a look."

***

Daphne had been busy playing with the tissue paper and had paid no attention to the man and his friends. She had decided that empty tissue paper was boring and had just curled into a ball inside the shoebox, when the door opened wide and light came streaming in. She blinked several times as her eyes adjusted to the sudden brightness. The man and his two friends were making that odd noise they did when something amused them.

"Well look at that. I'd say that's Schrodinger's cat."

"And it's in a box! Well done, Erwin."

The man added, "And at least we can tell that this cat is most definitely alive."

Daphne froze. Did that mean that this other cat the man had been talking about was dead? That didn't sound good, not good at all. She'd enjoyed her time with the man, but maybe she needed to get out while she still could. She would stay alert, and make a break for it when she had a chance.

"I was going to wait until I left," one of the friends said, "but as long as we're here at the coat closet..." He reached into the pocket of his coat. He fumbled for a moment, and pulled out something small, holding it out to the man.

"Go ahead, Werner. You can give it to her. That's why she likes you, you always bring her things."

The friend started to reach down to her, and Daphne prepared to jump away, in case this had something to do with whatever killed the other cat. But then she realized that the friend was holding a bit of cloth that had that catnip smell she liked. And she remembered that this friend often brought things like this. She extended her claws, reached up a paw, and snagged it out of his hand, which made the man and his friends make that odd amused noise again. She didn't pay attention as they partially closed the door, leaving her in the darkness, as she was too busy batting the catnip thing from one paw to the other.

Daphne began to feel very drowsy, just as she often did after playing with catnip things. She was vaguely aware of hearing the voice of the man and his friends in the other room. Sometime later she was distantly aware of the closet door opening, some coats being removed, and the front door opening and closing. She hugged her catnip with her paws, and started to drift off again, when the closet door opened wide. The man picked her up, and held her close.

"Come on Daphne, it's bed time."

He carried her into the bedroom, and placed her on the bed. A few minutes later, he began stroking under her chin. Daphne purred. Life was good here. Perhaps she'd let the man keep taking care of her for awhile longer. She could always look for the other cat tomorrow.

MR. MACCAWBER'S CHRISTMAS TRADITION

Roxanne Dent

CHRISTMAS EVE DAWNED chilly and bleak. A sharp, north wind whistled through St. Francis' small, neglected cemetery, carrying the last drops of rain in its wake.

It had been like this all week, Mr. MacCawber thought as he yawned and stretched, careful not to trip over the fallen headstones.

Mr. MacCawber was a cat. But he wasn't just any cat. He was a giant marmalade weighing in at forty pounds. He had topaz eyes, long, sensitive, fuzzy, pink ears, and feet as large and soft as a rabbit's, or so Professor Stieglitz was fond of saying when he was alive and Mr. MacCawber was his cat.

Professor Stieglitz loved Mr. MacCawber. Despite rules against burying animals in consecrated ground, he'd stealthily done so in the middle of the night. He visited Mr. MacCawber every Sunday, until he too passed on.

Before he died, Mr. MacCawber had never seen a ghost, human or animal, and didn't particularly want to be one. But before he became depressed at the idea of being a ghost, he discovered he had a talent in death he didn't possess in life. Mr. MacCawber could communicate with deceased humans. In 1872, there were a great many of them in St. Francis' Cemetery. When they learned Mr. MacCawber could talk, the human ghost residents were shocked. A talking cat! The very idea was outrageous.

But Mr. MacCawber was a good listener, gave excellent advice and could tell a spellbinding tale that cheered them all up, even on the loneliest nights.

It wasn't long before Mr. MacCawber discovered the humans who had been unable to fulfill their dreams in life remained ghosts the longest.

Occasionally, in the spring, when shafts of golden sun dappled through the budding leaves of oak and maple, and the birds sang their songs of celebration, Mr. MacCawber was convinced there was a special place animals went to after they were done being ghosts. After all, he saw grass grow again, trees that lost their leaves grew new ones, and humans eventually went to heaven. There must be a special place for animals, or perhaps they were born again. Until that day arrived, he made up his mind to be useful, and enjoy his status as resident Guardian of St. Francis Cemetery.

Licking his long, white whiskers, his topaz eyes gleaming, Mr. MacCawber looked forward to tonight. It was Christmas Eve and a tradition he initiated nearly 150 years ago was about to commence.

Sitting back on his haunches Mr. MacCawber cleared his throat and howled, "Rise up my friends. Rise up. It's Christmas Eve." This year, only two spirits answered his summons.

Miss Emily Vickers, wearing her favorite long black skirt, black boots, and white blouse, floated over. Her grey hair was piled up on her head, a cameo brooch at her throat, looking exactly like the spinster teacher she had been in 1887 when she died of pneumonia at forty-seven. She smiled. "Good evening, Mr. MacCawber."

Mr. MacCawber acknowledged her with a gracious nod. "Good evening Miss Vickers."

"I wouldn't like to be premature but I believe I feel a chill in the air that precedes snow. It would be nice to have a white Christmas."

"Indeed," Mr. MacCawber agreed.

"What now?" Jayne Barnett's shrill voice inquired sharply as her voluptuous form shimmered, before materializing in front of them with a pop. She wore a cheap red, silk, oriental dress with a slit down one side, her dyed black hair cut in an Asian bob, so popular in the 1920s. She snapped her gum in the irritating way she had and her blue eyes flashed.

"As you know," Mr. MacCawber began, "Every Christmas Eve, we help a live human to realize one of their dreams. This year that human is Ann Renault."

"Oh yeah, what's so special about her?" Jayne demanded. Mr. MacCawber sighed and his long, thick tail swished in irritation. Jayne still had difficulty seeing anything beyond herself and had to be cajoled into helping every year.

"Ann is in love with a man who doesn't value her affection," he explained. "An actor."

"Dear, dear," Miss Vickers murmured, distressed. "So sad, to love without being loved in return."

"I was in love with an actor once," Jayne put in, studying her long, red nails. "Very dishy, and he could play jazz that made you sizzle. Only trouble was, he was bone selfish. All he talked about was me me me, even when I tried to tell him about this show I was in. It was a Broadway show too." She tossed her black bob. "I mean, I wasn't just in the chorus, I was understudy to the star."

Mr. MacCawber's long pink ears flicked back and forth. If he had eyebrows like a dog he would have raised them. Really, the girl was impossible.

He took a deep breath before he continued. "Ann is a good, kind person who works hard as a nurse and volunteers at shelters. She has no judgment where men are concerned but she longs for love."

"Yeah, so who doesn't?" Jayne muttered.

Mr. MacCawber gritted his teeth, which were sharp as ever. "She's an orphan and wants a family of her own. It's not a lot to ask for, and she's always willing to give, unlike some," he added, turning his eyes on Jayne. "She deserves a loving husband who appreciates her."

"Blah, blah blah," Jayne snapped. "She sounds exactly like one of those namby, pamby, mealy mouthed do-gooders who knock on your door at some ungodly hour on Sunday morning."

"She's coming toward us now with her latest young man," Mr. MacCawber hissed. He made an effort not to lose his temper.

They all turned to look.

Ann Renault was in her mid-twenties. She was slim, with sandy colored hair, cut straight to her shoulders. She wore little makeup, and was dressed in jeans, a beige turtleneck, a short, beige jacket, and a soft oatmeal colored scarf around her neck. Beige was her favorite color.

Mr. MacCawber suspected Ann's love of the color beige was rooted in her own insecurities. Ann wasn't a stunning blonde or a flashy redhead, who could carry the bland color off. She didn't even have a tan. All that beige leeched the color from her delicate features. Mr. MacCawber felt Ann deliberately chose beige, so no one would notice her. It spoke volumes about her self-esteem.

Her companion had broad shoulders, lean muscles and stood just under six feet, with wavy, golden hair, blue eyes and a dimple in his chin. When he smiled, he had straight, very white teeth that showed up nicely against his tan. He sat down and Ann joined him.

"That cutie can't possibly care for her," Jayne sniffed, "with that tan and all that wavy, gold hair. A dimple too. He's mad hot. Why would a guy like that settle for a little mouse like her?"

"Hush!" Mr. MacCawber snarled, baring his needle-sharp teeth. Jayne hastily stepped away from Mr. MacCawber.

***

"You said you wanted to tell me something wonderful," Ann said gazing up into her beloved's eyes.

Eric glanced around the cemetery with a shudder. "I could have met you at a nice, warm café. You insisted on meeting here."

"Don't you remember, we met here a year ago Christmas Eve, but if you'd rather go someplace else—"

"No, forget it."

"So what's the exciting news?"

Eric squeezed her. "My new agent is a dynamo. I'm leaving for L.A. tomorrow to audition for a part on a sitcom. And she's lining me up with commercial work too."

"Oh Eric, that's wonderful."

"Those new pictures you paid for really helped. I'll pay you back once I get settled."

Ann moved out of his embrace. "You're not coming back?"

"L.A. is the only place for a serious actor. Vanessa swears I'll be a mega star in five years, maybe three."

"Vanessa?"

"I told you about V. She was in my method class. She introduced me to her agent who is now my agent. She's an awesome actress. She's going to L.A. too."

"You're traveling together?"

"We're sharing expenses. Everybody does it. Her uncle lives out there. He's a producer and promised to help us. We can stay at his place until we find something else."

"Oh."

"It doesn't mean we can't still be friends."

"I thought we were more than friends," Ann said tremulously.

Eric took her hand. "Look, Ann, we both had a lot of fun, but we didn't make any promises. I thought you'd be happy for me."

Ann removed her hand. "I am."

"Hey, don't be sad. I'll probably call you every night to ask your advice." He leaned in and kissed her lightly on the cheek. Her unhappiness was tangible. He stood up. "Look, I'd like to stay a little longer but I haven't even packed."

Ann nodded. "You'd better go. I want to stay

awhile."

Eric flashed his winning smile. "You can say you knew me when. I'll call you."

Once Eric was out of sight, Ann began to cry.

***

"Honestly, what did the little mouse expect?" Jayne exclaimed. "That guy's cool. She's as plain as vanilla pudding."

Mr. MacCawber felt like scratching Jayne's blue eyes out, or peeing all over her red dress. Of course, since she was a ghost, the stain wouldn't last. He sighed.

"Eric's not the first. Ann falls in love with men who use and then abandon her. What she needs is someone who loves her for who she is."

"Don't see how that's going to happen, given how she looks. I mean," Jayne added, hiding behind Miss Vickers as Mr. MacCawber ran toward her, his eyes flashing, "she could be smart as a whip and sweet as pie and even cook like a dream, but looks count with guys."

"I'm afraid Jayne's right, Mr. MacCawber," Miss Vickers agreed sadly. "Men can be kind, honorable, brave and intelligent, but most of them, especially the handsome ones, are also terribly shallow where a pretty face is concerned."

"Not all of them," Mr. MacCawber said. He looked off to the right of the cemetery, where a lone man was feeding the birds, a golden retriever at his side. The dog had no leash, only a harness, which the man held with one hand.

The man was tall, broad-shouldered, with thick,

black hair that fell over his forehead and the lean, firm body of a man who worked out at a gym on a regular basis. He tossed the last of the bird seed and turned away.

"Wow!" Jayne said. "My heart just went pitter-patter. He's got IT with a capital I. But what would he see in Ann?"

The man walked back to the bench very slowly, his hand firmly on the dog's harness. The golden retriever wore the kind of harness that belonged to guide dogs for the blind.

"That's Joe. Quick, we have to stop him from leaving," Mr. MacCawber yowled and rushed after the man and his dog. The others flew at his heels.

As Mr. MacCawber dashed across the cemetery he added, "The dog's name is Lattimer. See how he keeps looking back. He can sense us but can't see us yet. If we shape-shift into the most terrifying creatures we can dream up, and hurl ourselves at him with all the power we have, he'll see us as horrible monsters, turn tail and run in the opposite direction."

"You mean in the mouse's direction," Jayne said.

Mr. MacCawber could resist no longer, and bit her on the ankle as he passed.

"Ow!" Jayne shouted and tried to swat Mr. MacCawber. He was too quick for her, transforming as he flew. Having expanded his body to that of a ferocious, roaring lion, ready to snap off the dog's head, he went straight for Lattimer's nose with a huge snarl.

Prim Miss Vickers changed into a very tall, very scary vampire, with bloody fangs and burning red eyes. She reached out with filthy, long, black claws to grab Lattimer's harness, and roared as she did so.

Jayne gleefully morphed into a fire-eating dragon, fifty feet tall. She opened her huge, salivating jaws to hurl fire at Lattimer.

Poor Lattimer whimpered in terror at the attack of the three ghosts. He did exactly what Mr. MacCawber predicted. He turned tail and headed back toward the bench where Ann was sitting, his belly dragging along the ground, growling, barking, and whining in turn, his hair on end, and dragging his master along with him.

Puzzled at such unusual behavior from the well behaved Lattimer, Joe stumbled over his own feet. "Slow down, Lattimer. What's the matter boy?" The dog's whole body shook with fear. He howled, his soft brown eyes showing only the whites, his tail between his legs.

Ann looked up at their approach and dried her tears. "What's the matter with your dog? Can I help?"

"I don't know what's gotten into him. Lattimer's usually very well trained. He just freaked out. Do you see anything?"

Ann peered into the cemetery. It was twilight. She didn't see Mr. MacCawber, Miss Vickers, or Jayne. They had all returned to their former selves and were sitting on what was left of the marble headstone of a ship's captain who died over a century ago.

"I don't see anything. Maybe he senses a spirit. Animals have keener senses then we do. He's a lovely dog," Ann added. She knelt down and patted a trembling Lattimer. The dog kept nervously searching the cemetery for the horrifying entities who had pursued him and his master. Ann scratched him behind the ears and spoke soothingly. "It's all right, Lattimer. You're safe."

"Do you have a dog?" Joe asked after a moment.

"Pepper died five years ago. Now I have two cats. I found Loki wandering the cemetery last year. He was just a scrawny thing. Now he looks like Jabba the Hut. And Ra followed me all the way home from the grocery store one day. When I opened the door, he walked right in." She smiled. "I love animals."

"Me too." Joe paused. "Would you like to get a cup of coffee or something?"

Ann hesitated.

Joe tugged on Lattimer's harness. "Never mind." He started to turn away.

"I was wondering if the coffee shop around the corner is still open. I'm freezing. My name's Ann Renault."

"Joe Parizzi." Joe held out his hand and Ann took it."

She looked up and smiled. "It's starting to snow... I think it's going to be a white Christmas."

They walked off together, talking animatedly.

***

"So promising," Miss Vickers sighed.

"I suppose they live happily ever after in a little cottage with roses growing all around it?" Jayne grumbled.

"You can't fool me, Jayne Alexander," Mr. MacCawber said severely. "You get just as much pleasure out of these Christmas Eve events as we do. You just don't want anyone to know you're not as cynical and jaded as you'd like people to think."

"Tell us Joe's story, Mr. MacCawber," Miss Vickers urged.

"Joe proposed to his girl right over there under the

131

old maple tree last spring. It was right before he joined the Marines. He was sent to the Middle East, where he lost his sight when a bomb exploded. His girl broke off the engagement. He was very bitter and shut everyone out, old friends, family, everyone."

"She wasn't the right girl for him," Miss Vickers said firmly.

"He wasn't the same guy she fell for. Not everyone has guts," Jayne murmured.

Mr. MacCawber watched the couple walk down the block and disappear around the corner. "I followed him home one night and learned Joe planned on moving to Arizona after a cornea transplant. If he left without meeting Ann, it's unlikely their paths would have crossed. Christmas Eve brought them together."

"And a little judicious meddling," Miss Vickers added, her eyes twinkling.

Mr. MacCawber licked his paws and looked smug. "By the time Joe can see again, Ann will be beautiful to him. Because she'll feel loved, she'll glow with a beauty she didn't know she had."

"Yeah, well, she does have good bone structure," Jayne admitted grudgingly. "I hope the kids make it." She turned to Mr. MacCawber. "This year was an easy one, and more fun than a barrel of monkeys."

"Very satisfying," Miss Vickers agreed.

"I loved being a fire-breathing dragon and scaring a few years off that dumb dog," Jayne chuckled."

"We didn't even have to leave the cemetery," Miss Vickers added.

The church clock chimed twelve. "Merry Christmas," Mr. MacCawber called out as he leapt onto an angel, the largest stone edifice in the cemetery. It had been there even before he arrived.

"Yeah, Merry Ho Ho," Jayne added, as she yawned and whooshed away.

"Merry Christmas," Miss Vickers said faintly, her body already gone.

Thick flakes of snow began to cover the ground as Mr. MacCawber overlooked his domain from his perch high above. "Merry Christmas to all and to all a goodnight," he purred, as his ghostly form began to fade, his topaz eyes the last to vanish into the night.

A SILENT TRUTH

Meagan Noel Hart

NEARLY 200 PEOPLE ATTENDED Ethan Galton's funeral. Each of them had something to say about his wife, Eloise. I heard them whispering: *She's relieved. She only married the money. She'll replace him quickly, like she does her dogs.* Unleashed, I followed like a Great Pyrenees-shaped shadow. The crowd whispered about me as well. *Must she take that beast everywhere? She lacks heart and etiquette, bringing a dog to church.*

She didn't cry. Not when various colleagues and friends stood and shared their memories of him. Not when she spoke herself. Not when they put him in the ground. Her collected nature incited further gossip. Slander hidden by condolence. *You're being strong today, Eloise.* None of them were really her friends after all. Ethan had always been the social one.

I wanted to protect her, but I also wondered if they were right. Ethan and Eloise's relationship had always perplexed me. It was a mystery I feared I would now never know the answer to.

Finally free of the procession of judges, Eloise

relaxed in the limo. Despite the tinted windows, she squinted into the summer sun.

"It always rains in the movies." She ran her finger across the glass, tracing imaginary drops. "Life is seldom so poetic, is it Charles?" It sounded like something he would ask.

I thumped my tail in approval and moved my head onto her lap. I shed easily, and she was wearing black, so normally this would get a stern look at the least, but she ignored the transgression. My nose filled with her sweat and perfume, apricots.

Eloise and I were often in the limo alone, but knowing Ethan could never again join us unnerved me. I kept catching wafts of him. Lacquer, walnut, oak, and cherrywood. He owned a furniture empire, but his father had taught him to craft luxuries by hand from logs, and this was how he whittled away his free time. I already missed the sound of him chipping away in his workshop. When things went well, which they often did, it had an easy natural rhythm to it. Much like Ethan.

Ethan and I weren't particularly close, but he would share his toast and bacon with me. He was blunt, easy to read, and generally good to Eloise. He was a man a dog could trust.

We swayed a bit as the limo made a wide turn. Eloise reached for the golden dog whistle around her neck. She rarely used it any more. After nine years I could anticipate her needs and requests (even better than Ethan she once joked), but she always wore it. The whistle had been a gift from Ethan. Henry, the dog before me, had told me that. He explained a lot of things to me.

Henry was eleven, the top of our life span, when

Eloise brought me home. He eyed me, with my excited, awkward puppy's gait, and growled softly as I eagerly tried to introduce myself.

"So that's it," he had said. "She's already replacing me." Eloise only took in Great Pyrenees, he'd told me. The hope was I'd pick up some of his good habits before he died. An opportunity he hadn't had, as his predecessor had died rather quickly. I sensed resentment.

This wasn't what I'd expected.

When I weaned, my mother had promised I'd find love in humans. But according to Henry, I was a mere possession, interchangeable and moldable. Just an accessory. So, I decided if Eloise didn't have love to offer me, then I wouldn't care for her either. I resisted her training. She blew that gold whistle at me, for me, constantly. She was exasperated by my stubbornness, my refusal of her attempts at affection. I wanted her to give up and trade me in, but my refusal of her only seemed to make her more resilient. She was never cruel, only relentless. Looking back, I think Henry took some pleasure in our struggle.

It wasn't long at all before Henry died.

The day Eloise came to him and he didn't raise his large, shaggy head, she called for the maid. She related that he was gone, jotting some arrangements. Her tone offered no insight other than, "I was expecting this." It was what I anticipated. Cold, collected. Her motions were deft, and her demeanor suggested this was nothing more troubling than finding that a pair of pants was no longer in style. Then, she locked the door.

I was afraid she would turn to me, expecting me to be the dog she'd been trying to make me. Instead, she ignored me. She sunk to her knees and ran her fingers through Henry's thick fur, letting her fingers disappear. She lowered her forehead to his.

She cried.

Tears fell. Her chest heaved. Anyone passing in the hall would not have known. Her cries were as silent to them as my thoughts and language, but I could hear her pain in the soft whistles of her breath.

Slowly, I inched over on my belly and nosed her thigh. Without releasing Henry, or turning away, she reached one arm out, laying it gently down my back.

That was the true beginning of our relationship.

I paid attention. First, I learned her commands, her rules, the expectations. Then, I learned her movements, likes, dislikes, and habits. Her inclinations and moods, so wavering to others, to me became as reasonable as the smell of grass after a hard rain. I realized how seldom her words and actions matched the rhythms of her heart. Her true self rang to a tone only I seemed to hear. Our relationship became more than I had ever hoped for. It was direct and steadfast. If I displeased her, which was seldom, the anger was quick, the resolution simple. When she needed me, I was there. When I needed her, she responded aptly. It was intuitive, straightforward. Though I was not much older than when I first arrived, I realized how unreasonable I had been at first. Love at first sight was a fool's errand. I also came to realize that Henry wasn't trying to protect me from shattered expectations; he was trying to protect himself. His days were numbered, and he hadn't wanted to share.

I could hardly blame him.

As the years passed, I came to understand why I had been taken home before Henry died. It had nothing to do with training. I could never truly replace Henry, and she still would remember him fondly, but I could offer Eloise the same staunch love and acceptance that she could not go without. A constant loyalty and depth that she seemed to lack in other aspects of her life.

For me, our relationship was enough, but Eloise also had Ethan.

What he had to offer her seemed much different and much more dynamic. I couldn't exactly figure out his purpose. It was confounding and chaotic. Where I was rarely without her, he'd leave town for weeks on business, or work late into the night on a project in his workshop, not budging from his sanding or staining even if he promised to be to bed shortly. Yet there was no question he yearned to see her at the day's end.

At times she seemed as real with him as with me, her demeanor relaxing, her words flowing easily without pause, but at other times, she lied, distancing him. Sometimes I was certain she hated him. They'd slam doors and scream loud enough to cause me to hackle.

But, there were also times she'd sink into him like freshly turned earth. She'd return to me flushed and joyful, his scent wafting off her in thick waves.

It was a fluctuating, complicated cycle that I had learned to expect but couldn't hope to comprehend. There was something that bound them together, causing this interchangeable orbiting and colliding. Was this also love? The word was never said.

The limo turned again, bringing us further from the place of final goodbyes. I waited. Would she cry for Ethan as she had cried for Henry, as I knew she would cry for me? Did she regret not having a replacement for him waiting on hand? Or, had the whispers I instinctively wanted to protect her from all been true?

Was it Ethan who was just an accessory?

With care, she took the whistle from her neck. "This was his first gift to me, you know? Well, in part." She smiled. "He'd tied it to the collar of my first Pyrenees. He said my voice lacked authority, so I'd need something more." She scoffed. "He was never very delicate with words was he?" She clutched the necklace. The limo sauntered on. She pressed her other hand to the window. "He told me once he thought his funeral would be like the movies. Everyone dressed in black, standing in the rain, holding big black umbrellas." She looked down at me and smiled.

Then, her mouth loosened. For a moment, I thought she was going to say more.

She slumped forward, letting me hold the weight of her grief. I felt her chest heave first. Shortly after, her tears soaked into my fur. She clung to me, and I leaned further into her.

We finished the ride home in just this way, in silence.

Silence that told me everything I needed to know.

ABOUT THE AUTHORS

Amanda Bergloff
Amanda Bergloff is a speculative fiction writer whose stories have appeared in various anthologies, including *Stories from the World of Tomorrow, Frozen Fairy Tales,* and *After the Happily Ever After.* She is also an editor at *Enchanted Conversation: A Fairy Tale Magazine.*

Amanda lives in Denver, Colorado and collects vintage books, toys, and comics in her spare time. Follow her on Twitter:
https://twitter.com/AmandaBergloff

Ed Burkley
Ed Burkley is a Social Psychologist living in Oklahoma. By day he works as a professor and researcher studying human behavior at Oklahoma State University. By night he writes about the darker side of the human condition. His short fiction also appears in the forthcoming series *Night Shades* by Firth Books. He enjoys travel, photography, and spending lazy afternoons drinking hot cocoa in the backyard with his wife and Norwich terrier. www.edwardburkley.com

Roxanne Dent
Roxanne Dent moved to Massachusetts in 2000. She loves cooking, animals, movies, books and traveling to new places. She sold nine novels and

dozens of short stories in a variety of genres, including Paranormal Fantasy, Regencies, Mystery, Horror and YA. She has also co-authored short stories and plays with her sister, Karen Dent. Their most recent collaboration is a noir mystery, "The Werewolf Murders" for the anthology *Murder Ink,* Book 2, Plaidswede Publishing. The Dent sisters also collaborated on Book I, "The Death of Honeysuckle Rose". Roxanne is currently working on the novel, *The Grimaldi Chronicles, Beyond the Iberian Sea*, Book II in the Mick Grimaldi series about a shapeshifting NYC detective.

Member of New England Horror Writers (NEHW), Essex Writers and Artists Guild (EWAG), and Fiction Writers Guild (FWG). https://www.facebook.com/roxanne.dent www.thesistersdent.com

Sarah Doebereiner

Sarah Doebereiner is an author, editor, and avid reader from central Ohio. She graduated from Wright State University in 2010 with her BA in English. Macabre themes fascinate her because of their tendency to stay with readers long after the book closes. Sarah currently works for Claren Books as their Acquisitions / General Editor.

Connect with her via Facebook at https://www.facebook.com/sarahadoebereiner

Laurie Axinn Gienapp

Laurie Axinn Gienapp lives in northeastern Massachusetts with her husband and her two cats. She and her husband spend as much time as they can either ocean fishing or ballroom dancing. The cats spend as much time as they can, sleeping.

Her sci-fi/adventure novel *The Weatherman* was published in 2016, and the sequel is in the works. She has written a number of short stories, several of which can be found in the Read on the Run series. Frequently, but irregularly, Laurie posts to her blog at www.teapotmusings.blogspot.com http://lauriegienapp.com

Meagan Noel Hart

Meagan has been reading and writing stories all her life. Her work spans many genres and interests, though she is most known for her flash fiction and her focus on the individual and their unique place in the world. Her writing has appeared in *Welter, Everyday Fiction, Mothers Always Write*, and recently, Smoking Pen Press's *Unusual Pet Tales*. Her collections include *Twisted Together, A Short Stack of Silly Shorts for the Morally Sidetracked*, and *Whispers and Fangs*. She has an MFA in Creative Writing and Publishing Arts from the University of Baltimore. Besides writing, she enjoys designing the occasional book, baking fancy cakes, and playing with her kids and pets. By day, she's known as a Senior Lecturer at Stevenson University where she teaches writing and literature, including Video Games: The Art of Interactive Stories. http://mhart06.wixsite.com/mnhart

June Low

June is a freelance writer, part-time art student, avid cook, and bbq tenderfoot. Living in Los Angeles, she dreams of the rains in Seattle. On social media, you may find her on https://twitter.com/darthbunni or https://www.instagram.com/darthbunni/

Mary E. Lowd

Mary E. Lowd writes stories and collects creatures. She's had three novels and more than eighty short stories published so far. Her fiction has won an Ursa Major Award and two Cóyotl Awards. She tends to write about talking animals and spaceships. Meanwhile, she's collected a husband, daughter, son, bevy of cats and dogs, and the occasional fish. The stories, creatures, and Mary live together in a crashed spaceship disguised as a house, hidden in a rose garden in Oregon. Learn more at www.marylowd.com

R. J. Meldrum

R. J. Meldrum is an author and academic. Born in Scotland, he moved to Ontario, Canada in 2010 with his wife Sally. His interest in the supernatural is a lifetime obsession and when he isn't writing ghost stories, he's busy scouring the shelves of antique booksellers to increase his collection of rare and vintage supernatural books. During the winter months, he trains and races his own team of sled dogs.

He has had stories published by Sirens Call Publications, Horrified Press, Trembling with Fear, Darkhouse Books, Digital Fiction and James Ward Kirk Fiction.
https://www.facebook.com/richard.meldrum.79
http://wolfstarpublishing.com/meldrum/

Michael Penncavage

Michael Penncavage's story, *The Cost of Doing Business*, originally appeared in *Thuglit*, won the Derringer Award for best mystery. One of his stories, *The Converts* was recently filmed as a short movie, while another *The Landlord* was adapted as a play.

Fiction of his can be found in over 95 magazines and anthologies from seven different countries such as *Alfred Hitchcock Mystery Magazine* (USA), *Here and Now* (England), *Tenebres* (France) *Crime Factory* (Australia), *Reaktor* (Estonia), *Speculative Mystery* (South Africa), and *Visionarium* (Austria).

He has been an Associate Editor for *Space and Time* Magazine as well as the editor of the horror/suspense anthology, *Tales From a Darker State*.

Jonathan Shipley

Jonathan Shipley, a member of Science Fiction Writers of America, writes short stories and novels in the genres of fantasy, science fiction, and horror. In the writing profession, there are two huge challenges. One is the writing itself, and the second is getting the works published. In terms of output, he has written nine novels and over a hundred short stories. On the publication front, he has had over seventy short stories published since 1992, and one of the novels, a World War II occult thriller, is currently shortlisted by New York publisher Baen Books. Several more stories are sold and due out this year in anthologies and magazines.

A listing of his short stories can be found at www.shipleyscifi.com

Ginny Swart

Ginny is a South African who lives in Cape Town, and is the short-story tutor for three online writing colleges in South Africa, England, and New Zealand.

Her preferred occupation is writing short stories, and has over 700 accepted by magazines and anthologies all over the English speaking world. She has a couple of forgettable romance books out there too. She is still hoping to write The Big Novel but until then, shorts will do just fine!

www.ginnyswart.com

OTHER TITLES PUBLISHED BY SMOKING PEN PRESS

Links for digital and print versions of our titles are available from our website Smokingpenpress.com

Read on the Run series: Read on the Run is a series of anthologies with stories that are short enough to finish while you're going about your daily business, but long enough to tell a good tale.
> A Step Outside of Normal
> A Bit of a Twist

Other Anthologies:
> The Ancient

Novels:
> The Weatherman

If you need additional information please contact us or visit our website

E-mail: SPP@smokingpenpress.com
Website: Smokingpenpress.com

Made in the USA
Monee, IL
05 July 2021

72968571R00085